"I guess you're on your way to Silver City to find a saloon job, ain't you, girl?"

"No." Jessie's voice was cold. "I'm going to Silver City, but not as a prostitute or saloon girl..."

"Ah, you're just tryin' to run your price up!" another of the men growled. "Now, get off your horse and let's talk business!"

Jessie shifted in her saddle, and for the first time the men saw her holstered Colt.

"Not likely she'd be able to hit anything littler'n the side of a barn... Let's quit wastin' time!"

His hand moved toward his hip. Jessie's Colt was in her hand before he could reach the butt of his weapon...

Also in the LONE STAR series from Jove

LONGARM AND THE LONE STAR LEGEND
LONE STAR ON THE TREACHERY TRAIL
LONE STAR AND THE OPIUM RUSTLERS
LONE STAR AND THE BORDER BANDITS
LONE STAR AND THE KANSAS WOLVES
LONE STAR AND THE UTAH KID
LONE STAR AND THE LAND GRABBERS
LONE STAR IN THE TALL TIMBER
LONE STAR AND THE SHOWDOWNERS
LONE STAR AND THE HARDROCK PAYOFF
LONE STAR AND THE RENEGADE COMANCHES
LONE STAR ON OUTLAW MOUNTAIN
LONE STAR AND THE GOLD RAIDERS
LONGARM AND THE LONE STAR VENGEANCE
LONE STAR AND THE DENVER MADAM
LONE STAR AND THE RAILROAD WAR
LONE STAR AND THE MEXICAN STANDOFF
LONE STAR AND THE BADLANDS WAR
LONE STAR AND THE SAN ANTONIO RAID
LONE STAR AND THE GHOST PIRATES
LONE STAR ON THE OWLHOOT TRAIL
LONGARM AND THE LONE STAR BOUNTY
LONE STAR ON THE DEVIL'S TRAIL
LONE STAR AND THE APACHE REVENGE
LONE STAR AND THE TEXAS GAMBLER
LONE STAR AND THE HANGROPE HERITAGE
LONE STAR AND THE MONTANA TROUBLES
LONE STAR AND THE MOUNTAIN MAN
LONE STAR AND THE STOCKYARD SHOWDOWN
LONE STAR AND THE RIVERBOAT GAMBLERS

WESLEY ELLIS

LONE STAR

AND THE MESCALERO OUTLAWS

A JOVE BOOK

LONE STAR AND THE MESCALERO OUTLAWS

A Jove Book/published by arrangement with
the author

PRINTING HISTORY
Jove edition/December 1984

ISBN: 0-515-08055-1

Jove books are published by The Berkley Publishing Group,
200 Madison Avenue, New York, N.Y. 10016. The words
"A JOVE BOOK" and the "J" with sunburst are trademarks
belonging to Jove Publications, Inc.

PRINTED IN THE UNITED STATES OF AMERICA

Chapter 1

Jessie Starbuck was sleeping soundly in her bedroll, but she woke instantly to Ki's urgent whisper.

"Jessie!" he breathed. "Lie still! Don't move a muscle!"

Like everyone who has had frequent brushes with danger at the side of a trusted companion, Jessie obeyed the command. She did not even open her eyes, but her ears caught the tiny sounds of Ki's slow, cautious movements.

Fully awake now, and aware of the faint predawn light that filtered through the lids of her closed eyes, Jessie understood that some kind of danger was threatening her. She did not waste time wondering about its source, though they were on what should have been the safest place in the world, the broad prairie range of the Circle Star Ranch.

Jessie felt a quick breath of disturbed air pass over her face. She heard a muted sound, the impact of steel on flesh. So close to her ear that she could feel the air stirring against her cheek, she heard the sharp, high-pitched whir, the angry warning signal of a rattlesnake ready to strike. The whirring lasted only a few seconds, then died away in a series of spaced-out clicks and a light scraping of the snake's body on the hard, sunbaked earth. The rattles no longer buzzed in a sustained whir, but came in short, quick ticks lasting only a few seconds.

"It's all right now," Ki said, expelling his breath in a sigh of relief.

Opening her eyes, Jessie sat up. The rattler was writhing in its death throes only a hand-span from the spot where her head had been resting on the folded blankets of her bedroll. Its triangular head hung from its body by a thin thread of flesh, and its jaws still yawned wide, showing the tips of venom-laden fangs, as the muscles of its scaly diamond-patterned body spasmed in death. The snake was a big one, four feet or more long, its body larger around than Jessie's forearm.

"Thank you, Ki," Jessie said coolly. She nodded to indicate the gleaming, star-shaped *shuriken* lying on the ground a short distance beyond the snake. "That was a nice throw, when I think of the tiny clearance you had between my head and the rattlesnake's. I felt the wind as the blade passed my face."

"I had about a half-inch," Ki told her. His voice was quite calm and level, but his almond eyes were serious as he gazed past Jessie at the snake. It was still thrashing around, although each move was less vigorous than the last. He went on, "That's less than I like. And I couldn't move too much or too fast. The snake didn't rattle before it got to you. It was coiling to strike before I heard it moving."

Sun, Jessie's magnificent palomino stallion, was tethered only a few yards away. He had heard her voice and whickered now, a snort of greeting to his mistress. Jessie called to him, speaking his name, and Sun grew quiet.

While they'd been talking, the morning sky had brightened and the pink flush of sunrise was touching the rim of the horizon to the east. Details of the sprawling prairie were becoming visible by now, the tan earth showing at the roots of the short clumps of grass, the hump of an occasional rise beginning to cast its shadow in the brightening day.

"My stomach says it's time for breakfast," Jessie told Ki. She pushed away her blankets and fished her boots from the folds at the bottom of the bedroll. "By the time we get to the ranch, I'll really be hungry."

"Maybe we should've circled the arroyos last night and gone on to the main house," Ki said. He had already slipped out of his bedroll and pulled on his black, rope-soled slippers.

"No, we did the right thing." Jessie stood up and stamped the hard ground to settle her boots on her feet. "We'd have spent two hours going around. That would've been too much after such a long day in the saddle, and I wasn't about to risk Sun breaking a leg in the arroyos."

Ki walked past her to the rattler, which was now quiet except for an occasional twitching quiver, and picked up his *shuriken*. He wiped the thin steel blade clean on a tuft of grass and restored it to the vest pocket in which he carried the silent-striking weapons.

"Do you have anything planned for us to do, after the market herd starts to the railroad?" he asked. He dropped to his knees on the hard ground and began rolling up his blankets.

Jessie had already finished her bedroll. She said, "Not a thing. I'm so far behind in my desk work that I've got a full week to catch up on. And I'm only going to take care of any mail that's really important. Then I'm going to have a few lazy days just riding Sun around the ranch and resting."

"Alex always put off his desk work," Ki remarked as he tied the last string around his neat bedroll. "And the Circle

Star always came first when he was here, just as it does with you."

Jessie nodded as she and Ki began walking toward the horses. "I know. And he always rode a final inspection trip over the entire ranch after the hands finished the gathers. He said only the owner of a spread could see what even the best foreman might miss. But we didn't find a thing wrong, this time."

Alex Starbuck, Jessie's father, had created the vast Circle Star Ranch, which sprawled over most of three Southwest Texas counties in a spread bigger than some small European countries. Of all the properties Jessie had inherited from him, the ranch held first place in her heart, just as it had in Alex's. Though Jessie held the controlling strings of the vast business and industrial empire that Alex had woven together, the Circle Star was more than just a ranch to her. As it had been to Alex, it was home.

Approaching the two miles of arroyo-cut range that stretched ahead of them, Jessie took off her hat and hung it by its chin strap on her saddlehorn. They would be going slowly through the rough country, and would raise no dust; she enjoyed letting the morning breeze stream through her long hair, the hue of tawny gold, with just a shade more of copper than Sun's blond mane.

"I'm glad we didn't try to cross this in the dark," she told Ki as their horses slowed on reaching the first steep ridge. "I've thought about getting the hands to level it, working just a little at a time when they don't have anything else to do, but I hate to change anything on the Circle Star."

Ki smiled. "Yes. Your father said the same thing a dozen times about places on the ranch that are too rough and bare for the steers to graze on."

Jessie started to reply, then her full red lips tightened into a narrow line, and Ki realized belatedly that he'd reminded her of the rough section at the northeast corner of the ranch where Alex had died in an ambush, under a hail of lead from the cartel's hired assassins.

Jessie had stayed away from the Circle Star for more than a year following Alex's murder. The Circle Star had not seemed the same without him, so she'd thrown her energies into learning the details of the other Starbuck properties.

She and Ki had traveled constantly, visiting the Starbuck mines and timberlands in the Great Lakes region as well as those in the Pacific Northwest, the offices of Starbuck banks in California and New York, Pittsburgh, and Boston. Because no man of Alex's stature in the world of commerce could escape involvement with politics, she had spent some time in Washington, where President Hayes and his wife had invited her to dinner in the White House.

To acquaint herself with other companies in which Alex had substantial investments, she'd spent hours in the central offices of railroads and brokerage houses in the East. On the West Coast, she'd learned about the shipping line to the Orient and the import-export business that had been Alex's first large venture, financed by his success in the Oriental import store in San Francisco, where he'd made his start.

No matter where she'd traveled, Ki had been with her, tied by invisible strings of the loyalty he'd given Alex for having taken him in as a youth, when Ki had been driven from his own home by the stubborn prejudice of his Japanese family, which resented his half-Japanese, half-American parentage. As he'd been like a son to Alex, Ki was like a brother to Jessie. He'd been at her side during her battles with the vicious agents of the cartel, protecting her with his mastery of the Oriental martial arts that he'd learned from the master warrior, Hirata.

Jessie had inherited more than an industrial empire after

Alex Starbuck's murder. She had picked up the fight Alex had begun, thwarting the cartel's efforts to rob the United States of its industrial strength and its vast natural resources. It was a lonely fight for the most part, though fought on many fields.

Thoughts of the cartel were far from Jessie's mind as she and Ki let the horses pick their own path through the arroyo-cut stretch that lay between them and the Circle Star headquarters. They rode in a companionable silence that needed no words, until the rough country was behind them and they could see the main house and bunkhouse and out-buildings ahead.

"It looks like Ed has the herd shaped up," Jessie said, pointing to the mass of steers that filled the range at a short distance from the buildings. The shifting herd's shining horns caught the sunlight as the hands rode along its sides, bunching the cattle to start them moving toward the railroad spur, a long day's drive from the ranch. She went on, "I hope we haven't delayed Ed's departure by being late."

"It's not all that late," Ki said. "But here comes Ed to meet us, so we'll soon find out."

Ed Wright, looking tall and rangy even in the saddle, got to Jessie and Ki and reined in to match their pace.

"I hope you haven't been waiting for us to start, Ed," Jessie said as they let their horses set an easy walking pace toward the ranch buildings. "We stopped on the other side of the arroyos last night. Neither Ki nor I felt like crossing them in the dark."

Wright shook his head. "I was just sorta holding back till you and Ki got here, Jessie. Didn't know whether you wanted to ride to the spur with us or not."

"I'll think I'll pass, this time," she replied. "But Ki might want to go along."

"If you need me, I'll be glad to give you a hand, Ed,"

Ki said quickly. "If you don't, I'll stay here."

"Oh, me and the boys can take care of the size herd we got, Ki" Wright answered.

"Can you make it in a day, starting so late?" Jessie asked.

"Not and load out too, Jessie," the foreman said. "But we couldn't've loaded all the cars today anyways, no matter when we started."

"Will you take Gimpy with you, then?" Ki asked. "You'll need a couple of meals if you're not loading out until to-morrow."

"Oh, we'll do fine, Ki," Wright replied. "Gimpy's loaded up our saddlebags with sandwiches and cold truck, plenty to hold us till we get back. Besides, I'd as soon hold the critters at the spur tonight so's they'll be fresh for the train ride."

"You're sure the cattle cars got here?" Jessie asked.

"Setting on the siding," Wright nodded. "I sent Speedy up there yesterday to check up."

"You won't be back until late tomorrow, then," Jessie said. "Or will you be going all the way into San Antonio with the herd?"

"Not this year. I'll turn things over to Perk. He's a good enough segundo by now to be able to handle the job."

Jessie nodded. "Of course he is. And you've made the trip so often, I don't imagine it's much fun any more, even to get to see the bright lights."

"Now, you know right well I've had my fill of the Vau-deville Theatre and places like that, Jessie," Wright said as they reached the ranch house and reined in. "I'll be glad enough just to get the herd in the cattle cars and turn around and ride back home."

"Well, I hope you don't bring a lot of mail back with you," Jessie said. "I'm sure there's enough waiting for me now."

"More'n enough, I imagine. Speedy brought back a whole big bunch that he picked up when he went to check on the cars."

"Then you might as well move them out, Ed," Jessie said.

With a nod, Wright toed his horse into motion and started toward the herd. Jessie and Ki dismounted and wrapped their reins around the hitch rail at the side of the main house. Jessie looked over her shoulder toward the bunkhouse and dining hall.

"I think we'd better take our chances on a bunkhouse breakfast," she said. "I don't feel like waiting as long as it'd take for the stove in the big house kitchen to heat up."

"That suits me fine," Ki told her. "If there aren't enough leftovers to feed us, it won't take any time for Gimpy to stir up a mess of flapjacks."

"Let's go, then," Jessie said. "If I have to wait much longer, I'll be so hungry I'll start eating one of my boots."

Gimpy, whose full name was Thomas Jefferson Jones, though no one ever called him by it, was standing beside the big kitchen range with a cup of coffee in his hand when Jessie and Ki walked into the dining hall. He was a big man, his face showing signs that it had been very badly battered, either in one big brawl or a succession of smaller ones. He stood with his body at an angle because of the lame leg that had earned him his nickname.

"Morning, Miss Jessie, Ki," he said. "I sorta had me a hunch you two might be coming in, so I held back a little bit of batter to cook you up a batch of flapjacks."

"I'm glad you're a mind-reader," Jessie told him after she and Ki returned his greeting, "because I can't remember when I've ever been hungrier."

"Well, set right down," he invited. "And I'll have some grub in front of you before you get so weak you fall over."

Neither Jessie nor Ki wasted much time in conversation while they ate breakfast. Their hunger satisfied, they walked back to the main house. Evidently one of the two cowhands remaining at the ranch to take care of the daily routine chores had taken Sun as well as Ki's horse to the stable, for both animals were gone, the saddlebags Ki and Jessie had used during their checkup tour hung on the hitch rail. Ki lifted the bags and threw them over his shoulder.

"I'll take care of these," he said. "I know you're anxious to get to that stack of mail you've got waiting for you inside."

Jessie went at once to the big square room that had been Alex's study. Of all the rooms in the sprawling ranch house, it was the one she liked the best. In contrast to the the big rectangular living room, the study seemed almost cozy. A massive fireplace of slate-gray fieldstone dominated the pine-paneled room. Above the mantel hung an almost life-size oil painting of the mother Jessie had lost as a little girl. The wall opposite the fireplace was lined with bookshelves, crammed full of well-thumbed books. On the outer wall between two broad windows stood a small baseburner, with isinglass set in the pierced grille of its door.

All the furniture was scaled to the room's generous dimensions. A long, leather-upholstered divan stood at an angle that would receive heat from both the foreplace and the stove on a chilly winter day, and a smaller sofa, also covered in leather, faced it near the room's center.

The furnishings were completed by two leather-upholstered armchairs that would each hold two persons comfortably, and the scarred old rolltop oak desk that had been the first piece of furniture Alex had bought when he began his first store in San Francisco. There were, of course, small tables placed near the sofas and chairs, holding coal-oil lamps that at night cast a warm glow over the room. The mellow planks of oak flooring, the sheen of the leather, and the soft gold of the pine-paneled walls made the room friendly and inviting.

Jessie sat on the small sofa, rested her head on the soft leather back, and closed her eyes for a moment. A faint aroma of the cherry-flavored pipe tobacco Alex Starbuck had used reached her nostrils. She sat there for several minutes, eyes closed, quite motionless, her mind on what might have been. When she opened her eyes, the first thing she saw was the reality of today, the huge pile of mail on the desk, awaiting her attention. With a sigh, she stood up and moved to the chair in front of the desk, and reached for the topmost envelope.

Much of the accumulation of correspondence Jessie could put aside for more detailed study later, after making sure that it did not contain information or requests that required immediate attention. Most of it was material she received on a regular schedule, financial data from the Starbuck enterprises: operating statements, balance sheets, routine reports from the men who handled the day-to-day details of operating the firms.

There were letters from a score of charities to which Jessie contributed, following Alex's example, and these she gave only a fleeting glance before putting down. Some of the letters were social, for during her travels Jessie had made many friends. She'd almost reached the end of the heap when she noticed the yellow corner of an envelope that had slid from the top of the mail and slipped into the narrow slit below the pigeonholes that covered the back of the desk.

Fishing it out, Jessie ripped it open, and had just finished reading it when Ki came in. He saw the yellow envelope as he came to stand at the desk beside her.

"Not bad news, I hope?" he said.

Jessie shook her head, a small frown forming between the arches of her eyebrows. "I don't think it's really bad news, Ki. But it's too early to be sure. The wire's from Arthur Barston, at the First California Bank in San Francisco. I'm sure you remember him, we met him in Virginia City."

Ki smiled. "Yes, I remember the young man quite well. I'll never forget his expression when you asked him who owned the bank, and how he almost lost his voice when he had to tell you that *you* did." His smile fading, Ki added, "I hope the bank's not in trouble."

Jessie's frown vanished for a moment, and she shook her head. "I'm not worried about the bank, Ki. Morgan Willard wouldn't let it get into trouble, as long as he's the president. No, this telegram doesn't have anything to do with the bank."

"Then what's bothering you?"

Jessie's frown reappeared as she replied, "You remember that trouble we had at the Starbuck copper mines up in Montana?"

"Of course I do. That wasn't so very long ago, and we came out of it pretty well."

"But we spent a lot of time settling it," Jessie reminded him. "So after we got back from Montana, I wrote Morgan and had him put in a standing request with all his correspondent banks to notify him of any unusual mining activity in their areas."

"Maybe I could follow you better if you told me why that telegram has you looking so upset," Ki suggested.

"I'm sorry, Ki," Jessie said, and passed the half-sheet of flimsy yellow paper to Ki.

Ki read it, and as he did so, a frown similar to Jessie's formed on his own features.

CORRESPONDENT BANK LORDSBURG NEW MEXICO TERRITORY CONFIRMS MANY NEW SILVER STRIKES IN MIMBRES MTNS 50 MILES NORTH OF LORDSBURG.

REPORT ALSO SAYS EUROPEAN OWNED MINING
COMPANY CALLED MINERAL DEVELOPMENTS LTD
VERY ACTIVE BUYING CLAIMS PAST 2 WEEKS.
WILLARD.

Ki lowered the telegram and looked up at Jessie. He said, "I don't know what you think, but this smells like the cartel to me."

"It does, doesn't it?" She shook her head wearily. "Seems like we hardly get home before we're off again. Sometimes I wonder how much of this I can take."

Chapter 2

"Hadn't we better find out first if we're right about this being another cartel move?" Ki asked gently.

"Of course. I just haven't had time to check our records yet," Jessie replied. "I'd barely finished reading the wire when you came in. Offhand, I can't connect that company Morgan mentioned with any of the cartel's undercover operations, but it'll only take a few minutes to find out."

Jessie sat down and reached into the pigeonhole that only she and Ki knew concealed a latch which opened the secret drawer built into the desk. Her fingers tripped the hidden latch and the drawer opened. Lying on top of a stack of confidential reports and notes was the black leatherbound ledger in which Alex had recorded the confidential information his agents had uncovered regarding the history and activities of the cartel's top members.

Holding the book up, Jessie turned to face Ki. "If there's a connection between the cartel and this Mineral Developments, Limited, it'll be in here," she said. "And if the cartel is at work trying to get control of that new silver lode, you know what it means."

Ki nodded. "Yes. It means they'll be getting a lot of new

money to finance them in this country." He paused before adding, "It also means that you won't get those lazy days you were talking about, because we'll be leaving for New Mexico Territory as soon as we can pack."

Jessie nodded abstractedly, thumbing through the leaves of the dogeared notebook. She scanned each page quickly, reading Alex's flowing script with quick flicks of her eyes. At last she stopped and looked up at Ki.

"I think I've found what we're interested in," she said. She read from the book, speaking slowly because Alex had made all its entries in abbreviations, a sort of private shorthand. Now and then, when Jessie was stuck on a word, she had to stop and think for a few seconds before continuing.

"'Baron Ernst Josef Dolch,'" she read, "'Son of one of the founders of the cartel. Born Krefeld, Germany. Dolch money from shipping, steel mills, gold mines South Africa; silver mines Chile, British Columbia, Mexico. Married daughter of Lord Hershford, British cartel member. Hershford family also owns mining properties and smelters in Canada, Spain, Chile. Dolch and Hershford tried take over Hearst mines in Mexico, acting through jointly owned cover firm, Mineral Developments, Limited, headquarters London.'"

Jessie paused and looked up at Ki. "There's more, but this seems to be what we need to know."

"So it seems," Ki replied. He handed the telegram back to Jessie. "I suppose you'll want to start for New Mexico right away?"

"As soon as we can," she said. "We don't have any idea how long ago this Mineral Developments outfit began buying those silver claims before the bank in Lordsburg notified Morgan."

"I know where Lordsburg is, because we've been through it on the train," Ki said. "But we've never had any reason to go there before. We'll be going into unfamiliar country, Jessie."

"And rough country, as well," Jessie added. "But it won't be the first time, and I'm sure it won't be the last." She looked at the letters she'd put aside to be answered, and the reports and other material she still hadn't read. "I think I can finish these today. Ed and the boys will be back late tomorrow. Let's start the next day."

Ki nodded. "Whatever you say. Lordsburg's about a two-day ride on the train. But if we're going to have to travel into the mountains another fifty miles or so, we'd better take our own horses."

"Yes, of course. If there's really a big boom going on there, we might have trouble renting a pair from a livery stable."

"We'll have to ship them," Ki went on. "I'd take us the better part of a week if we rode."

"We won't have any trouble shipping them," Jessie said. "Sam Crane always has four or five cattle cars sitting on the siding at the depot. And usually a boxcar or two, as well."

"You'll take Sun, I suppose?"

"This time, I will. He needs to get the kinks out of his legs, and I'd rather ride him than any other horse on the ranch."

"I'll take that big pinto gelding," Ki said. "He's almost as big as Sun, and nearly as strong."

"We'll leave as soon as Ed and the boys get back, then."

Ki nodded. "While you're taking care of the paperwork, I'll get our gear together. And I think the first thing I'll do is have a talk with Gimpy. He was a saddle tramp before he hurt his leg and from the way he talks, he's been just about everywhere."

• • •

"Lordsburg?" Gimpy repeated when Ki asked him if he knew anything about the town or the country in its vicinity. "Up in New Mexico Territory? Why, sure, Ki. It's right down in the southwest corner, to the north of the Cedar Mountains, right between them and the Pyramids."

"I know about where it is, Gimpy," Ki said. "But I don't know what the country's like around it."

"Well, I guess I know it about as good as anybody. I was there afore Lordsburg was. That was afore I got my leg all gimped up."

"Is it cattle country, then? Prairie land, like we've got around the Circle Star?"

Gimpy shook his head slowly. "I misdoubt there's much in the way of ranches there. Might be some now, but there wasn't when I was prowling around in them parts."

"How long ago was that?"

"Why, that'd be right before the War, not long after I jined the army. Cavalry, a'course. First time I was thereabouts was with old Kit Carson's outfit. We was chasing the Mescalero Apaches, tryin' to herd 'em onto reservations."

"I don't think what you saw then would help much," Ki said. "That must have been almost thirty years ago, and the country around there is certain to have changed."

"Sure, the country's changed! Dagnabit, I done my part t' help change it! When I was in the army, there wasn't no such town as Lordsburg."

Ki saw that the only way to get the information he wanted was to let Gimpy ramble along in his own way. He said, "The part of that country I need to know might not have changed so much, at that. It's about fifty miles north of Lordsburg."

"I reckon it'd be pretty much the same as it used to be, that far from the railroad," Gimpy said thoughtfully. "But I was all over it, scoutin' out the Apache villages. Fifty miles north, that'd be in the foothills of the Mimbres Mountains, on aways past Big Burro Peak."

"Is it mountainous country, then?" Ki asked. "From what I could see out of the train windows going through there, it looked more like prairie. Pretty bare prairie, too."

"Oh, it is," Gimpy agreed. "Leastways, around Lordsburg. But there's mountains all around, that's why the railroad tracks winds like a running rattlesnake after they strike east coming outa Tucson. I oughta know, Ki. I helped build that railroad."

"I didn't know you'd ever worked for the Southern Pacific."

"Well, I didn't work for 'em very long. But about a year or so after I got my leg hurt, when I'd started cookin' on account of I couldn't fork a mustang no more, the SP needed a cook for their track gangs, so I signed up with 'em. That's how I happened to be on hand when Lordsburg was first started."

"Lordsburg's a railroad town, then?"

"I don't know as it is now. It sure was when it begun. It started out to be a division point, and a'course, Hell on Wheels moved along with the railhead."

Ki nodded. He was familiar with the mobile shanty towns that kept pace with the advance of railroad track construction. Housing a population of gamblers, saloonkeepers and whores, these villages had earned the name "Hell on Wheels" not only because of their rough and lawless inhabitants, but because many of the buildings had been constructed on bottom frames of heavy timbers that allowed them to be jacked up and fitted with wheels or skids and moved easily and quickly each time the construction crews advanced to a new railhead camp.

Gimpy went on, "Well, like I was saying, the tracklaying was held up awhile because the railroad surveyors hadn't made up their minds just how t' miss them mountain spurs that comes up from Mexico down in that corner of the Territory. A'course, the construction superintendent got all the blame for stopping. He was a limey, name of Lordsborough."

Ki broke in, "I think I can tell you what happened. The railhead stayed there so long that some of the people from Hell on Wheels put down roots and the camp turned into a town."

"You called the cards right, Ki," Gimpy said. "And the super's name was a leetle hard for them folks to handle, so they just cut it down to Lordsburg."

"It's an interesting story, Gimpy, but you still haven't answered my question. What's the country like to the north of the tracks? Prairie? Mountains? Forests? Desert?"

"A little bit of all them things," Gimpy replied. "Right around Lordsburg it's prairie, but the mountains begins a ways north. They're called the Gilas, but they ain't much but a spur of the Mimbres Range that starts up north a mite further."

"But what are the mountains like?" Ki persisted. "Raw, or wooded? Do they have good water, or are they dry?"

"Oh, there's water in the Mimbres. Used to be, anyways. The Mimbres River rises a ways east, and there's enough water so's they could build settling pits for them big copper mines they got up at a place called Santa Rita."

"I didn't know there were any mines near there," Ki frowned. "Copper, you said?"

"I guess there was a little bit of silver too," Gimpy said thoughtfully. "Most ever' place I been where copper's mined, there's some silver mixed in the ore. Them mines at Santa Rita's been there a long time. I heard that the old conquistadores that come there way back when was the ones that started 'em."

"Well, thanks a lot, Gimpy," Ki said. "I think you've told me what I needed to know."

"You planning to go up that way, Ki?"

"That depends on Jessie. She's thinking about it, and if she goes, I will too."

His voice holding genuine regret, Gimpy's said. "I'd give a purty to go along, but I can't pull my weight no more, not with my game leg, You know, Ki, that trail drive when Miss Jessie hired me on, it got bad in spots, but I guess it was the last fun I'll ever have." He added hastily, "Not that I don't like it here at the Circle Star. Miss Jessie's been real good to me, and you have too. But there's times when I do miss moseying around like I used to."

"Don't give up, Gimpy," Ki replied. "You never know, you might get a chance to mosey again. Not on his trip with us, but we might make another drive someday. And thanks for the information. It'll be helpful to us, knowing what to expect."

Later, after Ki had passed on to Jessie what he'd learned about the western part of New Mexico Territory, he said, "I got the idea from Gimpy that where we're going is still pretty wild, unsettled country. I'd say we ought to take along just about anything and everything we might need, including plenty of ammunition. You know how hard it is to get supplies in a boomtown where there's a big mining rush on."

"I'm not planning to be there very long, Ki," she replied. "All I had in mind was to look around and see if it's a really big silver strike, or just another false alarm."

"What about the cartel? Ki asked.

"I'm not going there with the idea of getting into any kind of fight, Ki. I just want to keep the cartel from getting another foothold."

"Do you think they'd be in there buying up claims if they didn't have a pretty good idea there was something solid about the strike?"

"No, I don't suppose they would," Jessie replied slowly.

After a moment of thoughtful silence, she went on, "I didn't really plan to stay there very long. But if we find there's any substance to the strike, I suppose I'll have to compete with the cartel in buying claims, and that would certainly bring on another fight. So when you start getting our gear together, maybe you'd better do as you just suggested, take plenty of everything. If it comes to a fight, we'd better be prepared."

The town of Sarah, Texas, had been built by Jessie's father and named for her mother. It lay not far from the Circle Star, and besides providing such limited amenities as a quiet town had to offer to local cowhands on a Saturday night, it also served as the Circle Star's link with the outside world through railroad and telegraph. Now, as Jessie and Ki stood in the town's small railroad station, Sam Crane looked out the station window at their two horses and turned back to them, shaking his head.

"I'm sorry as anything, Miss Jessie," he said. "I know you're in a hurry to get to Lordsburg, but the passenger train's more'n halfway here by now, and there's not anyplace along the line where it can couple on another baggage car."

"We'd lose a lot of time if we had to wait for tomorrow's train, Sam," Jessie said. "And Ki and I would have to ride back to the Circle Star and then come back here tomorrow."

"Oh sure, I can see it'd be real inconvenient," Crane said. "But like I explained to you, rules is rules. And the rules of the SP says we can't couple cattle cars to passenger coaches on a train making a regular run."

"Now, Sam, you know quite well there've been several times when you've put a passenger coach on some of the trains that hauled our cattle to the stockyards," Jessie said patiently.

"Uh-huh. But that ain't a regular run, Miss Jessie."

"Well, I don't see that putting a freight car on a passenger train is any different. And we need our horses with us when we get to Lordsburg," Jessie said.

"It's different, all right," Crane replied, mopping his brow for the third time since he and Jessie had been arguing. "Freights move a lot slower than passenger hauls, and freight cars or cattle cars just ain't built to handle that much speed. Their journals gets hot, and the wheel flanges has got a habit of busting when they run as fast as a passenger drag does."

"We don't want to cause any wrecks, of course," Ki assured Crane. "But as Jessie's already told you, we need our horses where we're going. We can't afford to lose the time we'd waste if we rode them all the way to Lordsburg, or had to wait for them to get there on a slow-moving freight train."

"Ki, if there was a way I could do what Miss Jessie wants me to, I'd sure do it," Crane said. "But it'd cost me my job if I got caught breaking the standing rules."

"I wouldn't expect you to break them, or risk your job any other way," Jessie told the agent. "But I've found there's a way to get around most rules without breaking them."

"I sure don't see how you can get around this one," Crane answered, pushing his cap back on his head to mop his brow with his shirtsleeve. "Horses is horses and people is people, and the railroad don't mix 'em together."

"Now, that's not quite right," Jessie said quickly. "I've had you ship Sun and other horses in a baggage car."

"That's true enough, Miss Jessie," Crane agreed. "But a baggage car has got the same kind of running gear as a passenger coach. So does them private cars like the nabobs have."

"A private car! That's it, of course!" Jessie said, more to herself than to Crane and Ki. She asked the agent, "You'd haul a private car if I paid your going rate, wouldn't you, Sam?"

"Why, sure. We haul a lot of them, even some of the high muckety-mucks at the SP main office has private cars."

"How much does a cattle car or a boxcar cost, Sam?" Jessie asked.

"I don't rightly know, Miss Jessie. I never asked nobody that kinda question."

I suppose you could find out in a hurry, couldn't you?"

"Sure. I'd just have to send a message to the purchasing agent in San Antone."

"You'd use the regular railroad telegraph, wouldn't you?"

"Of course I would, Miss Jessie."

"And he wouldn't be likely to talk to anybody about your question?" she asked.

"I don't see why. He's the boss of that department."

"He'd answer right away, too, wouldn't he?"

Crane shrugged. "It ought not to take him but a few minutes."

"Ask him for me, then," Jessie said.

Ki had begun smiling the minute he realized what Jessie was planning. To hide his grin, he turned away and looked out the window while Crane tapped the telegraph key. Jessie stepped over to join him while they waited for the reply.

In a whisper, Ki said, "Jessie, if you can make this trick work, you can get a fish to walk across the desert."

"It's the only chance I can see," Jessie replied. "Keep your fingers crossed until we get the car, though."

Five minutes passed, then another five, after Crane had sent his message. Then the telegraph key clicked and chattered briefly and the agent said, "Boxcars costs eight hundred dollars, Miss Jessie. Cattle cars costs six-fifty."

"I want to buy a boxcar, then," Jessie told him. "I'm sure my credit's good with your railroad, Sam. Just tell them to put the bill on our account."

"Now, Miss Jessie, if you're figuring—" Crane began.

"I thought you'd see what I have in mind," Jessie said. "So you might as well send a message to your trainmaster in San Antonio that you want the westbound passenger train to stop here and pick up Miss Jessie Starbuck's private car."

Jessie had gambled that Sam Crane was like anyone else who worked for a large company, and that he'd always welcome a chance to put something over on his bosses. When she saw the smile that flickered to his face, she knew she'd won the gamble.

"I don't recall anything in the rule book that says a private car's got to be a passenger coach," he said slowly. As he moved back to the telegraph key, he said over his shoulder, "Now, I'll be real glad to oblige you, Miss Jessie, but don't blame me if the conductor on that passenger drag don't feel the same way, and not want to couple up your car."

"We can worry about that if and when he does," Jessie replied. "Now go ahead and send those messages."

Jessie and Ki were sitting on the floor in the center of the boxcar as the westbound passenger train chugged up a gradual grade. They'd left the door just in front of them open a few inches, more to let a cooling breeze blow through the windowless car than to enable them to watch the countryside. At one end of the car, Sun and the gelding were tethered, munching grain from their nosebags. At the other end, Jessie and Ki had already spread their bedrolls and arranged their gear.

"I don't know how you manage to get your way every time," Ki told Jessie. "But it's certainly a good habit to get into."

"Don't give me too much credit," Jessie replied. "I've found that the Starbuck name helps a lot, and having the money to pay for what I want helps too."

Ki said, "The important thing is that we'll get to Lordsburg without wasting the week it would take us to get there on horseback."

"Of course it is," Jessie agreed. "And we'll be in better shape, too, that's one thing we can be sure of. If it comes to a fight, which it very well may, the cartel will try all the dirty tricks in their book. We're the only ones who know the danger the cartel represents, Ki. No one listens when we try to explain. We can't duck this job we've taken on."

Chapter 3

Standing on the platform of the freight depot at Lordsburg, waiting for the straddle-pallet that needed to be placed between the boxcar and the platform so the horses could be unloaded, Jessie looked at Ki and smiled.

"No wonder the station agent stared at me," she said. "If my face is smeared the way yours is with boxcar grime and cinders, we must look like Indians ready for the warpath."

"I wasn't going to say anything, but I imagine we both look about the same," Ki replied. "Traveling in a boxcar isn't exactly luxurious, but it saved us a lot of time."

Jessie glanced at the sun, which had traveled up the bright, cloudless sky toward noon. "I was hoping to get to the bank in time to catch the president before he leaves to have dinner," she said. "There wasn't much cash in the strongbox at the Circle Star, and I left most of it for Ed, in case he might need it."

"Why don't you go on, then?" Ki suggested. "I'll wait and bring the horses and our gear."

"That's the best idea," Jessie nodded. "I'll stop in the depot and wash, then go on to the bank. Before we start for the silver strikes, I want to arrange for them to honor any drafts I might have to write if we run short of money."

"Of course I'm familiar with your name, Miss Starbuck," Amos Roberts said, trying to hide his perplexed frown as he looked at Jessie's traveling costume of faded denim jeans and a loose blouse. "But I didn't ever expect to see you sitting here by my desk."

"Until a few days ago, I didn't expect to be in Lordsburg," Jessie replied. "But Morgan Willard in San Francisco wired me about your report of the silver strike up in the mountains to the north, and I decided I'd better come and find out what's going on up there."

"Ah, I see. And how may I be of service to you?"

Jessie smiled inwardly when she saw the banker's manner change from one of worried doubt to acceptance of her identity after she mentioned the name of the San Francisco bank president, something that only the real Jessie Starbuck would have known.

"I'm going up to the silver strike," she replied. "And I'd appreciate it if you'd tell me exactly where it is. I don't want to waste time looking for it."

"You won't have any trouble finding it, Miss Starbuck," Roberts assured her. "There's only one road north, and it leads you where you're going. It'll take you to the pass in the Mogollons that ends at the silver strike."

"Are there any landmarks we should look for?"

Roberts shook his head. "The road's well marked, though it's really more of a trail than a road. There've been plenty of wagons go over it, and there's a stagecoach running up to the mines twice a week now."

With surprise in her voice, Jessie asked, "Are miners actually working the lode so soon?"

"Oh, it isn't so soon, even if you've just heard about it. The first really rich lode was found almost two years ago.

The word got around at once—I don't suppose any news travels as fast as a gold or silver discovery—and the prospectors came flooding in. There's a town up there now, it's called Silver City. I haven't any idea how many mines are being worked; it seems that a new one opens almost every day."

"I see," Jessie said. "Now there's one thing more that I need to ask you about, Mr. Roberts. I left Texas in a hurry, and if I find some claims up there that look good, I may want to buy them. Is there a bank in Silver City?"

"Not a bank in the way you or I would think of it," Roberts replied. "There are two large merchants up there who do some banking as a sideline, but they don't always carry enough cash reserve to serve your needs, Miss Starbuck. By the way, in this part of the country, the miners don't call them 'claims.' They call them 'locations.'"

"But they're talking about the same thing?" Jessie asked. When the banker nodded, she went on, "I just wanted to be sure that your bank will honor my checks. You can clear them through the First California Bank."

"Why, of course we'll honor any check you write, Miss Starbuck! Without any question, and for any amount. I take it you're thinking of expanding your holdings by getting into silver mining here in New Mexico?"

"That'll depend on what I find," Jessie said. "So many of these strikes turn out to be false alarms that I won't know until I look for myself."

Roberts nodded. "I suppose you've seen enough mining to be a good judge. I know a bit about your family's interests."

"Oh, I'm not going to try to judge a silver lode myself," Jessie said quickly. "Before I left, I wired Morgan to hire a good geologist and send him here. He should be getting here in a few days, and I'm sure Morgan will have told him to ask your bank where he can find me."

"I'll tell my employees that any inquiries about you are to be referred to me," Roberts said. "And if we can be of any other service to you—"

"I'll call on you, of course," Jessie said, standing up. "Now I'd better get started north. Thank you for your help, Mr. Roberts."

Outside, Jessie found Ki waiting with the horses. When Sun saw Jessie, the big palomino began a feisty little dance of welcome and she stroked his soft nose to quiet him. Then she turned to Ki and said, "Let's look for a restaurant and have a good meal. Then we'd better load up on supplies, because from what the banker told me, we're going to a typical mining boomtown."

By the time Jessie and Ki started on the trail from Lordsburg to Silver City, the day was well along. Their path was well marked. The trail ran as straight as a tautly stretched light brown ribbon. It veered only to avoid the steepest walls of the arroyos that frequently cut across it, or to curve around one of the rock outcrops that reared above the hard-packed tan soil. When they'd gotten a short distance outside of town, they could see most of the ribbon as it ran across the level land until it was lost among faint patches of green, far upslope in the foothills of the Mogollon Mountains.

A few wagon-wheel ruts cut into the earth's thin crust made the trail easy to follow, but for the most part it had been marked by the hooves of horses, mules, and burros. Booted feet had left their prints where the dirt was softest, and along it on both sides was strewn the occasional common detritus that marks every advance made by civilization.

There were scraps of cloth and paper, an occasional pair of worn-out boots, an infrequent gleam of metal where some traveler had opened an airtight for a dessert of peaches or the food and drink that were combined in tomatoes. Shining shards of glass from discarded whiskey bottles were the most frequent signs of passage.

Except for an occasional stand of prickly pear or the thin sprawling stalk and trailing limbs of a cholla cactus, there was no vegetation. That lay ahead, visible even through the late afternoon's shimmering heat-haze. They made good progress across the long flat, as both horses were fresh and rested. When they started up the slope, the day was near an end, and their progress slowed as they started up the Mogollon foothills' southernmost spur.

Even when the sky reddened with the beginning of sunset, Jessie and Ki could see the green of small cedars and stunted pines on the crests of the foothills as they started up the long incline and began to look around for a suitable place where they could stop for the night.

In the short-lived desert dusk they found the spot they were looking for, a wide arroyo with a thick layer of white sand covering its bottom. A short distance off the trail, footprints and hoofprints, the windswept cinders of old fires, and a few heaps of ashes not yet scattered by the wind showed that it had been used before.

"It's as good a place as any," Ki said when Jessie pointed to the signs. "And we've certainly camped in worse."

Their night camp was made with the quick efficiency of experience. They tethered the horses with picket pins driven into the soft soil, and gave them a ration of corn in nosebags, then a scant few swallows of water. While Sun and the pinto ate, Jessie and Ki spread their bedrolls and ate a spartan trailside supper of the hard summer sausage and mellow yellow cheese they'd bought at Lordsburg. Then, after a final backward look showed them that the trail behind was as devoid of travelers as the rise ahead, they settled down to sleep.

• • •

Midmorning found Jessie and Ki making steady progress up the long slope that formed the next visible stretch of the trail. They'd risen at daybreak and were in the saddle before sunup. Now they could look back and see the ribbon of the trail over which they'd just traveled. Though it had been deserted the previous afternoon, clumps of travelers were now dotted along it, early starters just setting out from Lordsburg.

"It looks like we'll be riding alone again today, Ki," she remarked. "I suppose it pays to start on a trail like this at noon. Most people do what those down below there are doing, start in the morning, and travel in groups. I think I like it better this way."

They were moving more slowly now, keeping the horses fresh in anticipation of the climb's being a long one. The wisdom of their choice to conserve instead of hurrying was confirmed when they reached the spine of the ridge. They reined in to rest the horses, and looked ahead. To the north and south the mountains stood in a jagged array, their high peaks filling the horizon.

"That big peak just ahead must be the one Gimpy called Big Bear Mountain," Ki remarked as they emerged from the thick stand of pines through which they'd been passing. "All I can do is guess, of course, but it fits his description and it's the highest one in sight."

Jessie looked at the peak and said, "I can't see where the trail runs, but my bet is that it's going to get rougher as we get closer to the mines."

"That's a bet you'd be pretty sure to win," Ki said.

"I wonder sometimes about the men who make the first strikes in country like this," Jessie said thoughtfully. "What guides them to these places, Ki? Greed? Or just wanting to be moving all the time?"

"I wouldn't try to guess," Ki replied. "But we'd better

be moving on instead of sitting here. If we make those high peaks tonight, we'll be lucky."

By keeping the horses plodding steadily and eating in the saddle while the animals rested, Jessie and Ki passed through the rolling foothills and followed the trail up the base of one of the tall peaks just before sunset. Riding through the screening tree trunks, they emerged onto a shelf that ran from the side of one of the towering peaks to a drop-off a hundred yards distant.

At one end of the broad ledge they could see that the trail dipped precipitously down the mountainside. On the side of the cliff, between the trees and the edge, a spring discharged a trickle of water no bigger in diameter than a finger. The spring was almost hidden by the four men dressed in dirt-stained duck jeans and wrinkled flannel shirts.

They were unshaven rather than bearded. One wore a battered derby, and the others had on narrow-brimmed felt hats, all of which had seen better days. The one who wore the derby had a holstered pistol on his belt, but the others appeared to be unarmed. The four were so busy washing their hands and faces that they did not see Jessie and Ki for a few moments.

"Hey, we got comp'ny!" one of the men said as he turned away from the face of the cliff.

"Well, ain't that nice!" another exclaimed as he turned with his other companions to look at Jessie and Ki.

"And one of 'em's a woman!" the third man grinned.

"A woman that's got on pants, and a Chinaman with her!" the fourth said gloatingly. "Boys, I guess we all know what kinda woman that makes her. Looks like we'll have some fun tonight!"

Neither Jessie nor Ki spoke. The four men advanced slowly toward them.

Under his breath, Ki asked Jessie, "Do you want to ride

on and avoid arguing, or stay and deal with them?"

"I don't want any trouble," Jessie replied in the same half-whisper. "But we should stop here instead of trying to start down that trail. It looks treacherous, and it'll soon be too dark to see where we're going."

"I'll attend to them, then," Ki replied.

"No, Ki! Let me try to reason with them. There's no use fighting if we can avoid it."

A dozen feet from Jessie and Ki, the four men stopped. One of them said, "I guess you're on your way to Silver City to find a saloon job, ain't you, girlie? Or maybe you'll be looking for a vacant crib?"

"No." Jessie's voice was cold. "I'm going to Silver City, but not as a prostitute or saloon girl. Now if you're planning to camp here for the night, there's plenty of room. We'll camp at one end of the shelf, you can take the other. You men will stay at your end, we'll stay at ours."

"Ah, you're just tryin' to run your price up!" another of the men growled. "But you look close. You won't see no green in our eyes, girlie."

"That's right!" the first man put in. "No proper lady's gonna be wanderin' around wearin' pants, with a Chinaman in tow! Now get off your horse and let's talk business!"

Jessie shifted in her saddle, and for the first time the men saw her holstered Colt.

"Damned if she ain't carryin'!" one of them said.

"Not likely she'd be able to hit anything littler'n the side of a barn," the gun-wearing man told his companions. "Let's quit wastin' time!"

His hand moved toward his hip. Jessie's Colt was in her hand before he could reach the butt of his weapon. She triggered a shot, and the slug tore through the man's derby, sending it sailing from his head. He stretched his arms wide, hands spread open.

"Now hold on!" he yelled. "Can't you see we was just funnin' with you, lady?"

When Jessie did not reply, but kept her eyes fixed on them and her Colt's muzzle moving slowly, covering all four, the man who'd made the first mistake spoke.

"Yeah. We didn't mean nothin'. Maybe our joke was a little bit strong, but—"

Jessie cut short his stammered apology. "Which way are you men heading?"

"We're goin' to Lordsburg for grub. We been prospectin' up in the high country, but we didn't find nothin'."

"Then get on the trail again. You can go far enough before dark to find another place to camp," she told them, her voice cold.

"Now wait a minute, lady!" the man who'd worn the derby protested. "We're tired and hungry and we ain't—"

Again, Jessie asserted her authority. "I'd advise you not to waste time trying to talk me into changing my mind," she said. "And while I'm thinking about it, lift that pistol out of your holster very carefully and drop it on the ground."

"You ain't got no right!" the gun-toter said. His voice was almost a whine.

"I shot your hat off," Jessie replied icily. "I can shoot your holster off very easily, if you force me to."

Using his forefinger and thumb, holding the gun butt as though it were hot, he lifted the revolver out and let it fall to the ground.

Without turning her head, Jessie said, "Ki?"

He swung out of his saddle and stepped to the man's side. He picked up the gun and started to unload it, but Jessie stopped him before he'd slid the first cartridge out of the loading port.

"No, Ki. He's sure to have extra shells, and I don't feel like wasting time searching him. See if there's a tree over there with a high branch you can hang it on, a branch that's too high for them to reach without making a lot of noise, if they're foolish enough to come back for it before we leave."

Carrying the revolver, Ki walked toward the trees along the back of the shelf. He spotted a branch such as Jessie described when he was a dozen yards away. He ran a few steps, made a high leap, and caught a branch sturdy enough to bear his weight. Then he broke off a twig from a branch above it, and hung the pistol by its trigger-guard from the stub.

"Is this all right?" he called.

Jessie looked at the gun, saw that it was a good ten feet above the ground, and called, "That's just fine, Ki. Thank you."

As Ki dropped lithely to the ground, Jessie told the four prospectors, "Now get moving! You can come get your gun in the morning, but I'm a very light sleeper, and if I hear you prowling around here tonight, I'll shoot without warning. And I'd better tell you that I can hit a target as easily in the dark as I can in daylight."

"What about our gear? Our tools and grub?" one of them asked. "They're layin' over by the spring. We ain't et supper yet, and we been walkin' hard all day."

"Get your gear, then, and start out," Jessie said. "And remember what I said about coming back!"

"Don't worry, lady!" the gun's owner said. "We ain't plumb damn fools. We won't be comin' back here till we're sure you're long gone! And I ain't aimin' to git your dander up agin, but I got to say somethin' to you."

"Go on and say it," Jessie told him, trying to suppress a smile. "I'll hold my temper, if what you say isn't too bad."

"Now don't take me wrong," the prospector said. "We made a mistake when we taken you for a chippy. And you might not be no lady, either, but you're sure some hell of a woman!"

Jessie did not reply; she was afraid that if she spoke she'd start laughing. She nodded, and stayed on Sun while she and Ki watched the four go to the spring and pick up their knapsacks and their short-handled prospecting picks and shovels.

They started down the trail toward Lordsburg in the fast-fading light, grumbling to one another as they walked, looking back occasionally, until they were out of sight and hearing.

Ki said, "That was quite a compliment, Jessie. But I must say you earned it."

Smiling now, she answered, "I don't think we'll have to worry about them coming back tonight."

Ki shook his head. "No. You taught them a good lesson."

"I intended to," she replied. "Now let's get our own camp made and eat a bite of supper and turn in. If we get an early start and the trail's not too bad, we might get to Silver City before dark tomorrow."

Both Jessie and Ki slept lightly, but it was Ki who heard the sound and awoke first. As he sat up in his bedroll, his movements roused Jessie, and she was awake when the sound came again, so faint that it was almost inaudible.

"Someone's getting hurt!" she said. "A woman."

"Yes. Down the trail, in the direction of Lordsburg."

"You don't think those prospectors could've run into another party traveling, do you?" Jessie asked.

Ki frowned. "A party traveling with a woman? At this time of night?" He shook his head. "Not very likely, I'd say."

They sat listening. There was no moon, but at that high altitude in the thin, clear mountain air, the stars gave the sky a luminescence almost equal to moonlight. Along the face of the ledge, the trunks of the pine trees were clearly visible, even in the shadow of their branches. The trail they'd followed could be seen clearly until it entered the heavy foliage where it sloped down the mountain's broad flank.

They heard the sound again, a high-pitched cry, faint in the distance, that stopped almost at once. Jessie threw back her blankets and began pulling on her boots. Ki was already stepping into his rope-soled slippers. Both had turned in fully clothed except for their footwear.

Jessie stood up and strapped on her pistol belt. She said, "We can't stay here when we know someone's in trouble. Come on, Ki. Let's go!"

Chapter 4

Jessie and Ki strained their ears as they made their way quickly and silently through the belt of pine trees, but no more cries came from the downslope ahead. Beyond the pines there was a spot barren of any vegetation, and a short distance past it stood a clump of low-growing, bushlike mountain cedars. They moved across the bare expanse and were at the edge of the cedars when a yell rang out from somewhere beyond them. It was very near, and Jessie and Ki began running.

A man's voice reached them, calling, "Look out! The old son of a bitch has got a knife!"

Jessie recognized the voice as that of one of the prospectors. Immediately a second yell rang out, followed by a spate of words in a language she did not recognize.

"You hang on to the girl! We'll take care of him!"

This was the voice of another of the prospectors, Jessie was sure. The high-pitched yell rose briefly, then stopped abruptly.

Jessie and Ki were running now. They burst through the last of the cedars into a clearing, and saw the four men they'd chased away from the spring.

One was holding a woman, one arm around her waist, a hand clamped over her mouth. The other three were circling a small, stooped man. He was moving constantly, circling to keep his eyes on the three prospectors as they closed in on him. All that Jessie and Ki could tell about him in the gloom was that he wore a loose white jacket and trousers.

He held a knife in one hand and was waving it, the blade gleaming in streaks of dull silver as he slashed it in wide quick strokes, threatening the three men who were moving cautiously toward him, holding them at bay. None of the participants in the fray saw Jessie and Ki as they entered the clearing.

Jessie had her Colt in her hand, and was trying to find a line of fire that would not endanger the old man trapped by the trio of prospectors. Ki understood her problem after a quick glance.

"I'll take care of them, Jessie" he said, and almost before he'd finished speaking he started running toward the three prospectors and the old man.

As he ran, Ki tugged at the bow-knot of his *surushin,* a special rope wrapped twice around his waist in place of a belt. The knot came loose at a touch. The distance between him and the men who menaced the girl was not great, and Ki needed to twirl the *surushin* only three or four times to give it the momentum it required. One of the prospectors saw him and called a warning to the others, but Ki launched the *surushin* just as the man raised his voice, and the six-foot length of flexible rope with leather-covered steel balls at each end was already whirling through the gloom.

Before the shout of warning died away, the *surushin* had reached its target. The rope hit low on the prospector's chest, and the weight of the balls at its ends whipped them around his arms and body, holding him bound. The prospector forgot the man he'd been getting ready to attack and began twisting about, trying vainly to free himself, but he was unable to raise his hands high enough to reach the supple rope that held him tightly.

Ki was within striking distance of the prospector nearest him when the *surushin* found its mark. He knew that he had to incapacitate the man closest to him long enough to give him time to deal with the third opponent. He gauged his distance with the lighting judgment, by now almost an instinct, that had been instilled in him during his long period of training in the martial arts.

Bracing himself, Ki slid to a stop just out of reach of the prospector's outstretched hands. As the man facing him started to step toward him, Ki brought up his right foot in a snap-kick that smashed the foot into into the other man's crotch. With a howl of pain the prospector doubled up as Ki's upper instep thudded into his vulnerable testicles.

Knowing the pain would immobolize his adversary for several minutes, Ki whirled to face his last opponent. The fourth man was caught now between the knife-wielding man in white and Ki, whom he'd just seen put two of his companions out of commission in almost as many seconds. He held up his arms and began backing away, shaking his head, his hands held palm-forward.

"All right, Chinaman!" he said. "I give up! You don't need to worry about me! I got sense enough to know I can't stand up to nobody that moves the way you do!"

Both Ki and the third prospector had momentarily forgotten the man holding the knife. With a piercing yell, he lunged for the prospector who'd just surrendered. His knife hand was extended at waist level, the wicked blade thrusting toward the prospector's belly.

Ki's attacks had been carried out so swiftly that he had not yet lost the momentum of his running advance. He swiveled and lunged for the man with the knife. Sweeping his hand up in a *migi-shotei* blow, he brought the leather-hard edge of his hand upward to intercept the knife-wielder's wrist. The man in white grunted as the knife dropped from his numbed hand.

At the instant when Ki had launched his attack against the three prospectors, Jessie began moving toward the man who held the woman captive. His attention had been drawn by Ki's dash across the clearing, and he did not see Jessie as she silently stepped behind him and jabbed the muzzle of her Colt into the nape of his neck. He stiffened at the touch of the cold steel and did not move further.

"Let the woman go," Jessie said. She transformed her usually soft pleasant voice into a harsh, chilling whisper. "I'm sure you know what will happen if you don't!"

"You don't have to tell me twice, lady!" the prospector said. He released the woman instantly, and let his arms drop limply to his sides. "I told them damn fools you and your friend was likely to hear us if we jumped them 'Paches. I don't aim to give you no trouble. If there's one thing I can do without, it's a bellyful of lead!"

"Then go over to your friends and get them bunched up so I can cover all four of you easily," Jessie commanded. "I'm not anxious to shoot any of you, but I will if I have to."

Obediently the man started walking toward his companions. Jessie followed a step or two behind him. She was aware that the woman he'd been holding captive trailed along behind her, but did not risk losing her concentration on the prospectors by looking back or speaking.

Ki had pushed the white-clad man out of his way and was keeping his eyes on the prospectors. He and Jessie had carried out their attack so swiftly that the man entangled in the *surushin* was still trying to free himself. The one who'd received Ki's merciless kick remained bent over, his hands clutching his crotch. The third man still stood motionless, his arms held high, watching his companions and Ki.

"I want all four of you to pick up your gear and start moving again," Jessie said sternly, swinging the muzzle of her gun to keep the Colt a constant threat. "One of us might follow you down the trail, but you won't see us or hear us unless you try to come back. Now start hiking, before I decide you're not worth keeping alive!"

"Have a heart, lady!" whined the man that Ki had kicked. "I'm so sore I can't barely move, let alone walk!"

Jessie swung the Colt in his direction and said in a flat, unsympathetic tone, "I'm sure you'll find that you can, unless you want to be buried here."

Ki motioned toward the prospector who had not yet been able to get rid of the *surushin*, and told the man who'd given up without fighting, "Give your friend a hand. Just let my *surushin* drop to the ground when you untangle him." Seeing that the man did not understand, he added, "The rope. Get it off him and put it on the ground."

When the prospector started moving, Ki turned to the man in white. He said, "You and your lady had better move back to where you'll be out of the way if these men start trouble."

For a moment Ki thought the man had not understood him. Finally, with a guttural "Ha!" the white-clad man nodded and moved. Only then did Ki realize that he was an Indian.

Meanwhile, Jessie had kept the prospectors under her gun while they hastily scrabbled their few possessions together and started to move off. They maintained a sullen silence while they finished their tasks and started downslope, the man who'd taken Ki's kick still limping and groaning, one of the others half-supporting him. The quartet disappeared in the gloom, heading down the trail toward Lordsburg. Jessie waited until the sounds of their feet clomping on the hard earth had faded to silence, then turned back to face the others.

"Now that those rascals have gone, we can talk," she said. Her voice drew the two Indians toward her, but they approached slowly and stopped a pace or so away from her. Ki joined them after stopping to pick up his *surushin* and replace it around his waist. Jessie went on, "My name is Jessie Starbuck."

For a long moment the Indian man was silent, gazing at Jessie and Ki. He was old; his hair white, secured by a narrow headband, and he wore it in a long bob that reached to his shoulders and was cut in a clean, straight line at the bottom and above his eyes. The seams of age in his face started at his jutting chin, bracketed his thin, straight mouth, and crept like cobwebs over his cheeks and brow. He was not tall, standing an inch or two shorter than Jessie, but he held himself arrow-straight. Under the loose, belted blouse and full-cut trousers, she could see that his chest was both broad and deep.

"Sototo," the man said. He made no move to introduce the woman, who stood behind him, her head bowed bowed. Then he saw Jessie looking at her and added, "Her Ahi-té. She my *nieta*, baby my son."

When the girl lifted her head and bobbed it shyly, Jessie realized that she was quite young, Her hair was worn in braids that had been brought down her shoulders in front; her dark eyes, in the dim light, looked almost as Oriental as Ki's. Her nose displayed another Oriental characteristic, in that it was flat rather than aquiline, and her nostrils were quite rounded.

Her unbelted deerskin dress fell in a straight line from her shoulders almost to the ground, making it impossible to tell whether she was slim or fat. From her quick movements and erect stature, Jessie guessed that Ahi-té was in her middle or late teens.

"You're Apache, aren't you?" Ki asked Sototo.

Sototo nodded. "Mescalero. Medicine chief. My people

camp—" he waved his hand in a general northeasterly direction—"little way, there. We start to go camp, get dark, we stop. Men come, try..." He hesitated, peered up at Jessie's face, and said, "You know."

"Yes, I know," Jessie told him, wondering at the delicacy he showed in hesitating to utter the word *rape*.

"For my son, I thank you," Sototo went on. "I kill one, maybe two, you not come. But maybe not four. Too old, too slow now. In old days, I kill all."

"You were holding them off pretty well," Ki commented. "I don't know, you might have been able to handle all three of them."

Sototo turned to him and with a gesture indicated the throwing of the *surushin*. "Good," he nodded. "What people you from? Not *Diné,* not Hopi, not Pima. What people?"

For a moment Ki was stumped at the idea of conveying the idea of Japan to the old Apache. Then he pointed to the west and asked, "You know of the Big Water?"

Sototo nodded and said, "Hear about Big Water, not see."

"Far across the Big Water is my land," Ki went on. "It is called Japan."

Sototo grunted thoughtfully. "Good warrior, you."

"Thank you, Chief Sototo," Ki said. "From the way you were holding off those there men, I'd say you're a pretty good warrior yourself."

Sototo had no false modesty. He nodded and said, "Very good. All Apache good warrior. Fight from long time gone."

Jessie broke into their conversation. "Chief Sototo, don't you think it would be a good idea if you and your granddaughter came to the ledge where Ki and I are camped? I don't think those men will bother you again, but it would be better if we were together."

"Good," Sototo agreed. "You go. We come too."

Back at the ledge, the Mescalero chief looked around, saw the bedrolls that Jessie and Ki had deserted in such haste, and pointed to a spot at the opposite end, near the spring. He said a few words in Apache to Ati-hé, and she nodded and started in the direction he'd indicated. Sototo turned back to Jessie.

"We go early, you not maybe wake up," he said. "You do good thing to help Sototo. I do not forget."

With great dignity, he turned and followed Ati-hé to the spot he'd chosen as their sleeping place. Jessie turned to Ki.

"Chief Sototo seems like quite a man," she observed. "He certainly doesn't mince words, and he makes up his mind quickly."

"Yes. He reminds me a bit of my old teacher, who could still defeat his students in competition when he was eighty years old."

"Well, morning's going to come soon enough," Jessie said. "And I'd still like to get to Silver City before dark tomorrow. Good night, Ki."

"Good night, Jessie," Ki said, and, following her example, crawled into his bedroll.

Ki fell asleep at once and did not know how long he'd slept before he felt a touch as light as the wing of a butterfly brush across his cheek, then warm fingers pressed his lips tightly shut.

Opening his eyes, he looked up and saw Ati-hé bending over him. She tapped her own lips with the forefinger of her free hand and pointed to the shadows of the pine trees beyond the spot where the horses were tethered. Ki nodded. Ati-hé stood up and moved noiselessly away, heading for the spot she'd indicated. Ki slid from his blankets and, moving as silently as she did, followed her through the dim light. She was waiting for him in the blackness under the pine trees.

"I did not thank you when my grandfather was talking," she whispered. "It would not have been proper for me to speak until he gave me permission."

Ki was surprised at her almost unaccented English. He said, "You—"

"Speak English well, Ki?" she finished. "Of course I do. I learned when I was a small child, at the mission school."

"You didn't have to come and thank me," Ki said. "I just did what anyone would have done."

"No," Ati-hé replied. "No. Some men would have joined the ones who were trying to take me by force."

"I suppose they would," he said.

"Tell me something," she said after looking at him for a moment. "I have thought men from the other side of the ocean were all alike. But you are not like the Chinese I have seen working at laying the railroad tracks."

"I'm not Chinese. I'm Japanese. My people are as different from Chinese as yours are from the Kiowa or Comanche or people of the Pueblos."

"But you are very like my people in some ways," Ati-hé went on, gently tracing Ki's eyebrows with her fingertip. "You have Apache eyes. And you fight like one of our warriors." Her finger moved from the corner of his eye to his high cheekbones. "And our faces have the same shape."

"Who knows?" Ki asked. "Maybe our people came here long ago. We Japanese have sailed ships for more years than anyone can count."

"It may be so," she agreed. "But I did not wake you to talk about our people. I would like to lie with you, to open myself to you. Do you think this is a bad thing, Ki?"

"Of course not. But I don't want you to think you owe me a debt, just because I helped you and your grandfather."

"It is not to pay you for what you did!" Ati-hé snapped angrily. "It is something I want to do, for myself as much as for you! But if you would feel ashamed—"

"No," Ki said quickly. "That's not what I meant."

"Then come to me," Ati-hé invited, sinking to her knees

on the soft blanket of pine needles that carpeted the ground under the trees. She pulled her dress up to her armpits. "Show me that you are as good with a woman as you are in a fight!"

Ki knelt beside her. For a moment he looked at her body. It was slight, almost boyish. Her hips were almost boyishly thin, her breasts small, her pubic hair a black wisp between her thighs. Ki bent to kiss her, but before his lips touched hers, Ati-hé turned her head aside.

"You have taken up the round-eyes' habit! We Apaches do not rub mouths!"

"But do you do this?" Ki asked, bending to caress her breasts with his tongue.

"It is for babies—" She broke off, and Ki felt a tiny shiver run through her small body, then somewhat hesitantly she went on, "But I like it."

After a few slow, deliberate tracings with the tip of his tongue, Ki's lips told him that Ati-hé's nipples were growing erect. He continued his slow caresses, moving from one to the other until he felt her begin to quiver. Then Ki was aware of the pressure of her hands on his groin, working at the buttons of his trousers, freeing him, and then her fingers tracing the length of his erection.

She gasped. "You are bigger than most men, Ki!" Her hands closed over his jutting shaft and squeezed tightly. "I want you in me, now, Ki! Hurry, hurry!"

Ki rose above her quivering body and let her guide him into her. He sank down slowly in a long, deep penetration, and Ati-hé moaned, a throaty sigh that grew into short, urgent cries of pleasure as he began to stroke.

He did not hurry, but moved in a steady, deliberate rhythm until he felt Ati-hé's body begin to quiver and then to writhe, as she brought her slim hips up to meet his slow lunges. Then she was thrashing in a final frenzy, her small body shaking violently, one hand pressed over her mouth to stifle her throaty screams. She rocked and twisted for a few moments in her final ecstatic spasm, and then went limp.

Ki did not leave her. He pressed himself into her and held his hips close against her, still deep inside her. Ati-hé looked up at him, her eyes wide, as she searched his face in the deep gloom.

"You have not finished," she said wonderingly, then asked, "Didn't I please you?"

"Of course you did. But I haven't pleased you enough yet."

Ati-hé shook her head. "I don't understand, Ki. It is the place of a woman to please a man."

"In my land, it is also the place of a man to please a woman," Ki said. "Tell me something, Ati-hé. Have you been with many men?"

"Not many. Not as many as the fingers on both my hands. Why, Ki? Did you go to mission school too, where they teach that a woman must not be with a man unless words have been said for them to marry? That is not my people's custom, so we do not do what the mission school says we must."

"There are mission schools in my land too," Ki told her. "But we listen as little as your people do."

"Then why did you not let me please you?"

"So that I could please you more."

Ki started stroking again. He thrust as before, slowly and evenly, until he could feel Ati-hé's response beginning, then sped up and lunged with deeper strokes. This time he let his own frenzy mount with hers, until they gasped and shuddered and clung together in a long-drawn orgasm.

"Now I am sure that I pleased you," Ati-hé whispered. "But I still feel you as big as ever."

"That is something the men of my people learn, too," Ki told her.

"Aie!" she murmured. "It is something the men of my

people should learn to do!" Ati-hé squirmed from side to side, moving her hips gently. Then she asked, "And can you start at once again?"

"If you want me to."

"I do, Ki! Yes, I do very much indeed! And then again and again until it is time for me to go!"

Chapter 5

Jessie and Ki arrived in Silver City just before the sun dropped below the peaks of the Mogollon Mountains. In that mile-high elevation, the air was clear and soft, the sky just beginning to take on a twilight glow, but the softness of the waning light could not hide the little town's raw newness.

They came upon the main street by surprise as they rounded a sharp curve in the trail. It began abruptly with a livery stable on one side, a ramshackle rooming house and saloon on the other. Beyond these buildings, the rutted dirt street staggered at an angle across a gentle slope in a not-quite-straight line between structures that for the most part had been thrown together of raw, unpainted lumber. A closer look as they rode into town disclosed three or four brick buildings, all obviously brand new, two of them on a corner where a painted sign told them that Silver City's main thoroughfare had been named Broadway.

Signs of a boom were everywhere they looked as they rode on slowly through town. In a half-dozen of the open spaces between the stores and saloons, carpenters were busy at work on a number of new buildings in various stages of completion, and on some of the older stores there were also men working on additions, upper floors, new fronts, or extensions at their backs.

As they rode up Broadway, keeping close to one side to avoid the occasional wagon or rider that passed, Jessie and Ki noticed that a number of the commercial buildings consisted of a false front of lumber with a tent extending behind it. In a few cases a storekeeper had avoided even this much time, trouble, and expense. Instead of buying lumber and hiring carpenters to erect a false front, they'd simply fastened a canvas sign bearing the store's name above the entrance of a big tent.

Though darkness was still an hour or so away, the dancing flares of kerosene jug-lights were already sending up ribbons of black smoke in front of a number of buildings. There were a few wagons on the street, and a number of saddle horses and packmules, and the board sidewalks were covered with men. Most of them wore the duck pants and flannel shirts that were favored by prospectors and miners, and a majority of them were bearded or badly in need of a shave.

They'd almost reached the opposite edge of town when Jessie pointed to an approaching wagon and said, "Ki, there must be a sawmill somewhere close. Look at that load of lumber."

Ki followed her finger and saw the big-wheeled lumber wagon, its flat bed piled high with boards so freshly sawn that the odor of pine pitch reached them as the vehicle passed by. They watched it until it reached the end of the street, turned off past the livery stable, and disappeared.

"There are plenty of pine trees around here, Jessie," Ki said as they toed the horses ahead. "I wouldn't be surprised if some of the men who came here without knowing anything about prospecting gave that up when they got discouraged, and decided to make lumber instead."

"Mining takes a lot of lumber for shoring and things like

that," Jessie said thoughtfully. "If there's a big demand for it, I'd take that to mean the silver lode must be a good one. And if it's a good lode, I don't think I'd like to see it belong to the cartel."

"Finding out how good it is shouldn't take very long. Then you can decide exactly what you want to do," Ki told her as they moved on.

They reached the point where the business buildings gave way to long, narrow structures on each side of the street, buildings with closely spaced doors above which red lanterns had already been lighted. They rode on past the cribs and reined in their horses. The slopes extending from Broadway were fully visible now. While the buildings stood in fairly orderly rows for a short distance on each side of the wide main thoroughfare, those on the slopes were scattered like raisins on top of a layer of well-stirred batter. On the side of the upslope just behind Broadway, a pair of large two-story frame buildings rose above an unruly gaggle of small houses, shanties, and tents covering a large triangular area that stretched up the gentle grade and ended at a sharp ridge.

A creek that showed as a silvery thread as it wound down between the houses from the crest explained the reason for the shape the settlement had taken. Each newcomer had built as close as possible to the running water, while later arrivals had been forced to put their houses farther away. At the top of the triangle, the small cabins near the crest of the ridge stood only two or three deep. These highest cabins gleamed with the bright yellow of newly sawn lumber, while those at the bottom had weathered to a gentle orange hue.

On the downslope side, an even larger frame building dominated the smaller houses that nestled around it beyond the street. These formed a shallow rectangle with its longest sides parallel to the thoroughfare. On both upslope and down, the houses, shanties, and tents beyond Broadway were perched with no sign of orderly arrangement, but were scattered in a higgledy-piggledy array. Beyond the last houses on the downslope side the creek spread wider, then vanished in a wide expanse of rush-covered, marshy-looking land.

There was some movement around the houses. Behind one of them a woman was carrying a pail to a well, another was hanging wash on a line, and two or three pairs of trios of gossipers were standing around chatting. At one house a man was dismounting from a horse; at a few of the others men were repairing walls or windows or loafing on doorsteps. Two or three groups of children were playing in open spaces between the dwellings.

"Have you noticed the same thing I have, Ki?" Jessie asked.

"If you mean the little adobe ovens, it would be hard to miss them. There's one behind almost every house," Ki replied.

"And you remember where we saw so many of them before?"

"Of course. In Mexico. In Oaxaca, where there are so many little silver mines. The miners use them for smelting."

"If every miner has a little smelting oven, there must certainly be plenty of silver," Jessie went on, gazing back along Broadway. Then she added, "The town doesn't look like very much, but boomtowns never do. I've seen enough of them in the few years I traveled with Alex to understand that."

"Yes, I remember them too. And I've gone back a few years later to some of them, and they've turned into orderly, neat towns."

Jessie went on thoughtfully, "After what we've just seen, I think the best thing we can do is to get a half-mile or so away from town and camp. I'd say that upstream along the creek would be our best bet."

Ki nodded. "I didn't see any sign of a hotel, but I imagine

those three big buildings at the back of the street are rooming houses. We might find rooms in one of them."

"From their looks, we'd be better off in a tent."

"Which we don't have," Ki observed.

"No, but I'm sure we can buy one," Jessie said.

"If we knew how long we'd be here, I could build a little shanty of some kind," Ki suggested. "This high in the mountains, there's usually some rain at night the year round, and you might find a tent uncomfortable."

"We'll think about a building when we know how long we're going to stay," Jessie said.

"Let's ride back to the livery stable, then," Ki suggested. "I imagine it's the stagecoach stop—it usually is, in a town like this. Then we can find a restaurant. You're probably as tired as I am of eating cheese and sausages three times a day."

"A change would be good," Jessie agreed as they reined the horses around and started back down Broadway. "We'll take the other side of the street and look as we go along. Maybe we'll see one that's more appealing than the others."

They'd ridden only a short distance when Jessie said, "We missed something when we were heading the other way. Maybe because there were too many men standing around it. Look at that little new building, at the sign on it."

Ki saw a small, narrow, hutlike building that had been squeezed between two larger structures, one a saloon, the other a doctor's office. It was so new that its boards still shone pristine yellow. A sign over its door read, LOCATIONS BUYER. CASH FOR PROVED STRIKES.

"You think it's the cartel's buyer?" he asked Jessie.

"That wire I had from Morgan Willard said they've been very active the past few weeks."

"There's no name on the sign," Ki frowned. "How can we make sure it is the cartel?"

"If it is, we'll find out soon enough." Jessie turned in her saddle to look back at the building. Then she swiveled around to face Ki and said, "Let's rein in here, Ki. A man just came out, and I want to see where he goes."

Pulling over to the side of the street, they stopped and waited. The man Jessie indicated was walking slowly toward them, pausing to look in the door of each store he passed.

Frowning thoughtfully, Jessie said, "I might be making a mistake, Ki, but he looks like a miner or prospector to me."

"Yes, he does. Have you got something in mind?"

"I was wondering, if I just went up and asked him, whether he'd tell me if he's sold a claim—a location, that is. Not everybody would feel like talking freely to a stranger."

"If he's sold a claim at a good price, he'd be feeling so good he'd enjoy telling almost anybody about it."

Jessie's frown deepened. "It just occurred to me that he might work for the cartel."

"He doesn't look like the kind of man who'd be working for them, but I suppose you can't tell much at a glance."

"No, you can't judge by his looks, Ki. But what bothers me is that anybody working here for the cartel would be warned to be watching for a woman who came around asking questions."

Ki thought for a moment. The man was only a few paces away from them by now. He said, "Suppose I ask him? There are a lot of cartel men who'd know about a woman named Jessie Starbuck, but I'm not that important. Besides, anywhere you go in mining country, there are a few Chinese prospectors and miners."

"I can't say I agree with you about your not being important, but he might talk to you a little more readily than he would to me," Jessie said thoughtfully. "Go ahead, Ki. Ask him."

Ki dismounted and stepped to the sidewalk. He waited

until the man reached him and said, "Excuse me, sir. Would you mind answering a question for me?"

"A question? What about?"

"I saw you come out of that place up the street where they buy mining claims," Ki said, improvising as he walked a fine line between truth and fiction. "If I was to try to sell a little strike I made up in the hills, do you think they'd give me a fair shake?"

"What makes you think I sold them a location?"

"I was just guessing," Ki said. "I supposed anybody who came out of there had been selling. I'm sorry if I was wrong." He turned as though to leave.

"Wait a minute," the man said. "I don't reckon it'd hurt me to tell you. I sold my location to 'em, all right."

"Did they beat down your asking price much?"

"No." The man frowned and went on, "I guess maybe they didn't try to dicker me down on account of I been working it for about five months now, and its still producing pay dirt."

Ki realized instantly that now that he'd broken the ice, he might get even more information. He asked, "Did they give you cash for it, or a check drawn on some bank back East?"

"Well, they give me a check, all right, and I asked 'em how I knowed whether or not it was any good, because I didn't much want to take it. It's a foreign outfit, see, but they said they'd fixed it up with all the saloons and some of the stores so I could get cash for it right here in Silver City, and not have to go all the way to Lordsburg, or maybe even to Las Cruces."

Ki twisted his face into a worried frown and asked, "Was the name of the company on the check? Or was it just a plain piece of paper signed by somebody you never heard of?"

"Oh, its got the company's name on it, all right. Some

outfit over in England, called Mineral Developments. That fellow in the office was a limey, or talked like one. He said their main business is buying up a lot of little working claims like mine. Then, when they got enough, they turn 'em into one big dig, like the one over to the east at Santa Rita. I just showed the man some assay reports I got back from El Paso, and he paid off like a faro dealer. Didn't hardly dicker at all after I told him I had my price set in my head."

"I won't take up any more of your time," Ki said. "Thank you for telling me what you found out. I guess it'd be all right for me to sell to them."

"Seems to me it would, if that's what you wanta do. Me, I'd rather work a location till its proved good, then sell it fast and go stake out another one. It beats swinging a pick all day."

"Good luck," Ki said. "I hope you strike it rich."

"Same to you," the young miner replied as he turned away.

Ki went back to Jessie and the horses. He said, "It looks like the cartel's really busy, Jessie. That miner had sold his location and they'd paid him with a check. I don't need to tell you the name on the check, I suppose."

"If it was anything but Mineral Developments, Limited, I'd be surprised," she replied.

"It was. And that fellow said the man who seems to be in charge of buying talked like an Englishman." As he mounted his horse, Ki added, "Your banker in San Francisco gave you good information."

"Morgan's information is usually good," Jessie agreed. "And I don't think whoever's acting for the cartel would put up a sign like that unless they had enough information to know that this strike is more than just a flash in the pan."

"We'll stay here, then, I suppose." Ki's remark was a statement, not a question.

"Yes, Ki," Jessie replied firmly. "We'll stay here until we've beaten the cartel. We've done it before, and we'll do our best to do it this time."

"Of course we will," Ki told her. "But before we start fighting them, shouldn't we find a restaurant and eat supper?"

"Did either of those three cafes we saw look any better than the others?"

Ki shook his head. "They all looked about the same to me."

"Let's just go to the one across the street, then," Jessie suggested. "While we're eating we can decide whether we want to ride out from town a little ways and camp, or see if we can find rooms in one of the rooming houses."

Reining their mounts around, they started across the street. They'd pulled up at the hitch rail and were starting to dismount when another wagon loaded with lumber passed on the street behind them. Jessie settled back in her saddle and watched it for a moment, then turned to Ki.

"Even if we're both hungry, I want to follow that wagon, Ki," she said. "I've been thinking about your suggestions to put up a little one-room shack, and I think it's a good one."

"I can wait to eat," Ki said. "Let's go buy lumber."

Just as the wagon they'd seen earlier had done, this one rumbled to the end of Broadway, and turned behind the livery stable. Jessie and Ki had almost caught up with it by the time the wagon left the road, and they were only a short distance behind it when the teamster reined in, dropped off the seat, and went into the house where he'd stopped.

Guiding their horses around the wagon, they pulled up at the hitch rail. The door stood ajar, and they could hear the rumble of voices inside as they pushed it a bit wider. When the light from the room beyond flooded the front of the door, Ki nudged Jessie and pointed to the sign they hadn't been able to see before. The sign bore the legend, TOWN MARSHAL. COME IN.

He whispered, "Either the marshal's charging the teamsters to unload, or he's buying himself a lot of lumber."

"We'll soon see," Jessie whispered. She knocked on the doorframe.

"What's the matter, can't you read?" a man's voice called. "Come on in."

They stepped inside, into the lamplight, and saw at once why the house had been so sturdily built. Iron bars partitioned off one end of the long room to form a cell. At the other end stood a rolltop desk, a cot, several chairs, and a tall woodstove. A man sat at the desk, and another stood in front of him. Both were looking toward the door when Jessie and Ki got inside.

Jessie recognized the man standing as the teamster they'd followed, and paid no attention to the one sitting at the desk. She asked the wagoneer, "You just brought that load of lumber into town, didn't you?"

"Sure did, lady. Why?"

"Because I'd like to buy it from you, if it's yours to sell. And if it isn't yours, I'd appreciate it if you'd tell me who to see about buying it," she replied.

"Well, it ain't mine," the man told her. "Wisht it was, 'cause everybody's looking for good fresh-cut pine boards. But if you wanta buy the load, you can talk to that feller right in front of you. It belongs to him."

Turning to the man at the desk, Jessie said, "I suppose you're the town marshal, but we just got here and I don't know your name."

"I'm him, all right. And the name's Nolan, Tate Nolan."

Jessie sized up the marshal with a single quick, perceptive glance. Nolan was a big man, beginning to run to belly.

For all his size, his hands were so large that they looked out of proportion to his body and head.

He still had on his hat, and Jessie could tell nothing about his hair color, but imagined it would be black, for his eyebrows were thin black lines of only a dozen or so hairs apiece, set above eyes of such light brown that when he turned his head they faded and looked yellow, like those of a cat. Nolan's cheeks and chin were clean-shaven, but he wore a thick, swoopingly curled mustache that gleamed in the lamplight with macassar oil. His cheekbones were set high, but his jaw was narrow and tapered to a point. He sat sideways in his chair to accommodate the bulge of his holstered revoler.

Jessie went on, "Then, as I told this other gentleman, I'd like to buy that wagonload of lumber from you, Marshal Nolan."

Nolan shook his head. "I'd like to oblige you, but it's already sold. The way things are around Silver City, there ain't enough lumber hauled in to keep the carpenters busy."

"You'll be getting another load soon, I suppose?"

"Oh sure," Nolan replied. "O'Grady, here, and his partner hauls in about six loads a week."

"Then I'll take the next wagonload," Jessie said. "If you'll just tell me how much a load costs—"

Nolan broke in, "Every load that's coming in here for the next two months is already spoke for by somebody that's been here a lot longer'n you have."

Jessie had inherited Alex Starbuck's persistence. She said, "Perhaps one of the men who's bought one of those loads would like to make a quick profit. If you'll give me their names and tell me how to find them, I'll be perfectly willing to pay—"

"I'll say this for you," the marshal interrupted, shaking his head. "You're sure stubborn as—" He stopped short, then went on, "You sure got a mind of your own, Miz—"

"Miss," Jessie replied. "And my name is Jessica Starbuck."

"Miss Star—" Nolan began, then stopped short. His eyes narrowed as he continued, "Miss Starbuck. Well, I'm afraid I can't accommodate you. I don't want somebody running around making my customers mad. Looks like you'll just have to wait for your lumber. I don't know when I'll have a load I could sell you. Might be quite a while."

Both Jessie and Ki had observed the change in Nolan's manner after she'd told him her name. They exchanged glances, and with the understanding created by years of close companionship, they had no need to say anything. Jessie shook her head, a motion so slight that no one but Ki would have noticed it.

"I'm sorry to hear that, Marshal," she said levelly. "I don't suppose there's any need for me to stop in again in a day or two and see if there's been any change?"

"No need at all," Nolan replied curtly. "The folks here in town gets first call on all boards that comes in. Might be a year or more before I got any to sell strangers."

Jessie nodded. "I see. I won't take up any more of your time, then."

She turned and left the office, followed by Ki. They went to their horses and swung into their saddles without speaking. Only when they were well on the way along the road leading back to the livery stable did Jessie speak.

"Was the smell of something rotten as strong to you as it was to me back in the marshal's office, Ki?" she asked.

"Very strong indeed. It began when Nolan heard your name."

"Yes. And both of us know what that smell means. The cartel hasn't just been buying up locations here in Silver City. Somewhere along the way, they bought the town marshal too."

Chapter 6

"If that geologist doesn't get here soon, one of us will have to ride back to Lordsburg and send Morgan Willard a wire, asking what's happened to him," Jessie said.

She and Ki were standing at the hitch rail in front of the livery stable. It was the same place they'd stood for the last two days on which the stage for Lordsburg was scheduled to pull in. The investigations they'd made of several small one- and two-man silver mines in the vicinity had convinced Jessie that there were other lodes, perhaps even a main lode comparable to the Comstock, which had not yet been discovered.

Even though their inspection of the locations had been superficial, Jessie was increasingly anxious to start buying those that showed promise, and perhaps even to start the geologist searching for new locations.

"Forgive me for reminding you again of the old saying my people have, that the journey of a thousand miles begins with one small step," Ki said. "We have done all that we can, and if our step seems small, at least we've begun."

"I know, Ki," she replied. "I keep telling myself to be patient, but every time we've come into town, we've seen two or three men go in or out of that location-buying office. If we could get out hands on the lumber we need, I'd be tempted to open one of our own, as close to theirs as I could get."

"We were lucky to find that little tent we're camping in," Ki reminded her. "It hasn't rained yet, but when it does, we'll be glad we've got shelter."

After searching through all the stores in Silver City, they had found only one tent. It was small, and so far they'd had to use it only once, during a small early-morning shower. Being familiar with the unpredictable weather of the high Western mountains, marked by sudden heavy rainstorms, they knew that a gullywasher could strike without warning at any time and flood their camp on the ridge above the town.

"I suppose I want to do too much too fast," Jessie admitted, "But the cartel has enough of a start on us now, and I don't like to run second in any kind of race."

"We're not—" Ki began.

He stopped abruptly when a high-pitched yell sounded from the rear of the stable, followed by an excited babble of raised voices. They stepped to the corner of the building to look for the source of the commotion, and saw a knot of men at the far end of the stable, where it joined the corral fence.

"Whatever's going on, it's none of our affair, Jessie," Ki said. "But I suppose we'd better go see what the fuss is."

They started walking along the back of the stable. The men at its corner were spread along the pole fence of the corral now, shouting and waving. Jessie and Ki reached the point where the stable and fence joined, and could look into the corral. They saw an old Apache man, his back against the end wall of the stable, waving a long iron rod to keep at bay a half-dozen white men who were darting at him singly and in pairs, trying to grab the rod.

"That's a branding iron he's holding!" Jessie exclaimed.

"Yes, and it's hot," Ki said. "No wonder they don't want to grab the free end. It's still glowing red!"

One of the onlookers heard them and turned to explain, "He come in tryin' to sell a old crowbait horse. When Sharkey told him he didn't want the nag, the old feller got riled up. That branding iron was in the forge gettin' hot, and he grabbed it and taken after Sharkey."

Another quavering war whoop from the old Apache broke the air, and the man who'd been talking to Ki and Jessie turned back to look at the affray going on in the corral. The liveryman and his helpers were using a new strategy. Splitting up, two on one side and three on the other, they'd begun working their way along the wall, forcing the Indian to turn away from one group in order to watch the other.

"That old fellow's a real fighter!" Ki exclaimed. "Five of them against him, and he's attacking!"

"From what I've seen and heard, Apaches never give up," Jessie said. "I don't see why they keep pushing him. All they'd have to do is wait until the branding iron cools, then they could get it away from him easily."

For a moment the old man swiveled his head furiously as he tried to keep both sets of the livery stable workers under observation. Then, as the pair approaching from his right side were almost ready to reach out and grab him, he feinted quickly toward his left and jumped spryly away from the wall.

Turning as he landed, the old man scraped the smoking end of the long branding iron along the wall. Smoke rose as he scraped the hot tip along the wall and forced the two who'd been on his right to join the other three in the corner where fence and stable joined.

For a moment the five men crowded into the corner, pressing back as the branding iron sizzled in the air, inches from their faces. The old Apache loosed another of his war whoops as he waved the rod back and forth.

His coup was short-lived, though. The penned livery stable workers ducked between the fence poles and pushed through the onlookers, separating as they moved along the fence, and crawling through the fence poles back into the corral well past the end of the stable. Forming into a rough quarter-circle, they started advancing on the old Indian again.

"Don't get too close to him!" one of them warned. "That iron's still hot enough to take the skin off of your hands!"

"That's right," another called. "Just keep him cornered. I sent the flunky after Tate Nolan, he'll be here in a minute."

Nolan arrived almost before the man had finished speaking. The marshal pushed through the spectators, listening to their excited descriptions of what had happened. He'd turned his eyes toward the corral at once and had not noticed Jessie and Ki among the moving, chattering spectators. Keeping his eyes on the cornered Apache, he ducked through the pole fence and, after waving the liverymen back, drew his revolver.

"Surely he's not going to shoot him!" Jessie gasped.

Nolan called, "Drop the iron, old man!"

When the Indian did not obey, but responded with a shrill yell of defiance, Nolan put a slug into the livery stable wall just beside his head. For a moment the old Apache hesitated. Then he tossed the branding iron as far as he could toward the center of the corral and held his hands outstretched, palms up.

"That's better," Nolan said. He lowered his revolver, but held it dangling beside his thigh instead of returning it to his holster. His lips curling in a wolfish grin, he went on, "Now start walking away from the wall. Come on over here where I am, but damn you, stop when I tell you to stop!"

In a half-whisper, Jessie told Ki, "He's putting on a show!

Why doesn't he just arrest the old man if he's going to, instead of humiliating him?"

"You've seen his kind before, Jessie," Ki said. "You know why. A man like him lives to impress anybody who's looking."

After he'd stared at Nolan's angry face for a moment, the Indian started slowly forward. He'd taken only a step or two when Nolan's revolver cracked and its slug plowed into the ground only an inch or two from the old man's foot. He stopped and locked eyes with the marshal. Nolan waited for a moment, then when he could see that the old man was not going to move, he repeated his earlier command.

"Damn you, I told you to keep walking!" Nolan shouted to the Indian. "Don't stop till I give the word!"

This time the old Apache obeyed. He'd taken only one step forward when Nolan's pistol barked again. This time the bullet raised dust close to the Indian's other foot.

Outside the corral fence, Jessie had gasped when Nolan fired his first shot, but when the second shot split the air she turned indignantly to Ki. In a half-whisper she said, "Let me have your *surushin,* Ki, quickly!"

"Jessie, you're not planning to—" Ki began.

She cut him off. "I'm not going to hurt anybody. Just give me the *surushin.*"

Ki undid the knot with a single tug and unwound the rope from his waist. As he handed it to Jessie he asked, "Would you like for me to throw it?"

"No. I'm not as good with it as you are, but I'll fry my own fish, Ki. Thanks just the same."

While she spoke, Jessie was whirling the *surushin* above her head. She let it fly and it sailed toward the marshal. Nolan was facing the old Apache and did not see the *surushin* flying toward him. It struck him at his waist and the two weights carried its ends around his hips and twirled them back on each other. Nolan was trapped, his gun hand pulled tightly against his upper thigh, his left forearm bound to his waist.

"What the hell!" Nolan barked, trying to pull his arms free and failing. The last twirl of the weighted ends had locked the *surushin* firmly, and it resisted all his efforts to pull free.

Jessie had started pushing her way through the crowd the moment she was sure her throw had been a good one. Ki was a step behind her. The men who were watching from the area outside the fence were standing silently, gaping at Nolan's struggle to free himself. Their surprise was at least equal to that of the town marshal's, for they stepped aside absently, still gazing at Nolan, not even turning their heads to see who was pushing up to the fence. When Jessie halted at the corral fence, Ki stopped as well. He said nothing when he saw her draw her Colt.

Nolan did not notice Jessie for a few moments; he was too busy trying to break free of the *surushin*. When the men at the fence began moving away from her, the marshal looked up. He saw her watching him, and scowled.

"Damn it, are you the one that threw this—this—" He began, then spluttered into an apoplectic silence.

"It's called a *surushin,* Marshal Nolan," Jessie replied coolly. "I doubt that you've ever encountered one before. It won't do you any good to try to break free, but if you'll step over here to the fence, I'll take it off."

Nolan's face was almost purple by now. He stared at Jessie, as though trying by sheer force of will to make her come to him, but when she stood calmly waiting, he began walking toward her. She let him take two steps, then casually lifted the Colt she'd been holding at her side and, without seeming to aim, put a bullet into the ground beside his foot.

At the report of Jessie's gun, the men around her began to push back. They started talking to one another, a low buzz of excited babbling.

Nolan had flinched when the bullet whistled into the earth at the side of his foot. He stopped walking again and snapped, "Be careful with that damned gun! You might hit somebody if you don't look out!"

"I only hit what I aim at, Marshal," Jessie replied. "But I told you to come over to the fence. Perhaps I'd better give you a reminder."

Again she fired offhand, not appearing to aim, and again the slug from her Colt plowed up the earth only an inch or two from his foot. Nolan had learned quickly, though. He jerked his foot forward at once and continued walking toward the fence.

After Jessie's second shot and the brief exchange between her and Nolan, the tone of the onlookers' voices changed. A few snickers and one or two outright guffaws could be heard from the men pushing up to the fence. None of them spoke out, though, and none of them moved to stop Jessie.

"What're you up to, anyhow?" Nolan asked as he neared the fence. "I guess you know I can arrest you for interfering with a law officer!"

"Of course you can arrest me, Marshal. And I'd like nothing better than to stand up in court and testify to how I gave you a taste of your own medicine," Jessie said sweetly. She holstered her Colt. "Keep walking, Marshal Nolan. I won't draw my gun anymore, so there's nothing for you to be afraid of."

This time Jessie's retort drew more than a few guffaws from the onlookers. There was a bit of goodnatured shoving as the men crowded closer to hear what she and Nolan were saying.

"I'm not afraid, damn you!" Nolan gritted as he stopped at the fence.

"Why, no one said you were," Jessie said mockingly. She reached between the poles and took Nolan's gun from his swelling hand. "I'll just make sure you won't be tempted to do anything you might regret when I get your hands free."

Jessie flipped open the loading port and pulled the hammer of the Colt single-action back to half-cock. She twirled the cylinder, found the two live rounds and poked them out with the ejector rod, then placed the weapon in the marshal's holster.

"Now turn around, and I'll free your hands. Just remember that I still have three rounds in my gun," she said, leaning forward to unwind the ends of the *surushin*.

Nolan stood glowering at Jessie as she finished removing the *surushin* and handed it to Ki. He rubbed his wrists without taking his eyes off her. She kept her face expressionless, and did not allow him to lock eyes with her. This time the laughter from the men crowding outside the fence was louder and more general.

Jessie was having trouble keeping her face expressionless, trying not to smile. She glanced at the old Apache, who still stood motionless in the corral. He was watching Nolan and Jessie and the crowd with his obsidian-black eyes, his face showing no emotion whatever. The men watching were quiet now. Some of them were smiling broadly at Nolan's humiliation, and the faces of a few of them were twisted into puzzled frowns, as though they sensed the animosity flowing between Jessie and the marshal, but did not quite understand what was going on.

Jessie asked Nolan, "What did the old Indian do to justify your shooting at him, Marshal Nolan?"

"How in hell would I know?" Nolan asked, anger still grating in his voice. "The flunky from the stable came running into my office and said there was an Indian going crazy over here. I did what any other lawman would, I came to stop him."

"So you really didn't know whether he'd broken the law or not when you fired at him?" Jessie asked, her eyebrows lifting in mock surprise.

"Oh, he broke the law, all right," a man called from the crowd. "That's why I sent for Tate."

"Go ahead, Sharkey," Nolan called. "You own this place. Go on and tell the lady what the old redskin did."

"He was stealing my horse-corn and eating it," Sharkey said. "He come in and tried to sell me a skinny old nag that ain't fit for nothing but glue. I told him I didn't want to buy no hoss that looked like that one, and forgot about him. I figgered he'd go away, but after while I seen him dipping into the cornbin and eating my corn. I told him to skedaddle, and give him a little shove, then he pushed by me and run out, past where Luke was heating the branding irons. He grabbed up one when he went past, and that's when I sent the boy after the marshal."

"How much corn did he eat?" Jessie asked.

Staring at Jessie, Sharkey blurted, "How in—" He stopped short and started again. "I don't rightly know. But he might've been feeding that nag outta the bin before I seen him."

"You didn't *see* him feed the horse, though?" Jessie prodded the livery stable owner.

"I told you what I seen, lady," Sharkey replied. "That's all I know, except that I seen him trying to fight off my men with that branding iron."

"Well?" Nolan asked quickly. "Does that satisfy you, *Miss* Starbuck?"

"It satisfies me that you were making a fool of yourself, Marshal," Jessie answered. She turned back to Nolan. "I think you charged me fifteen cents for a bushel of feed corn the other day. Am I right?"

The liveryman nodded. "That's my regular price."

Jessie dug a handful of coins out of her pocket and handed Sharkey two dimes. "Give the old man a bushel of that corn, and keep the change to pay you for what he took."

"Now hold on!" Nolan blustered. "That old devil's going to jail!"

"I suppose you could charge him with fighting or something of that sort," Jessie said. "But if you do, I'll see that when he's tried he'll have a lawyer, or I'll be there myself to defend him. If you put him in jail, I'll post bail for him. You'll be going to a lot of trouble for nothing."

"What's that old booger to you?" Nolan frowned. "As far as I know, you never set eyes on him before."

"I didn't. But I hate to see anybody, Indian or Mexican or white, get a raw deal," Jessie replied levelly. "Now have you changed your mind about arresting the old man? Or will we settle things in court?"

Nolan hesitated. Jessie could see that he was thinking of the way he'd been made to look foolish a few moments earlier, and wondering what surprises she might have for him in a courtroom.

"All right," he said grudgingly. "He didn't hurt anybody, and whatever corn he stole has been paid for. I don't guess I'll haul him in, as long as Sharkey's satisfied."

"I ain't got any quarrel with the old fellow," the livery owner said quickly. "This whole thing don't amount to a hill of beans, anyhow."

Seeing that there would be small chance for further excitement, the spectators began drifting away. Jessie stood quietly, her eyes fixed on Nolan. He met her level gaze angrily for a few moments, then took a half-step back and flicked his eyes around. The only remaining spectator was Ki, who stood leaning idly on the corral fence a few feet away.

"I've heard a little bit about you, Miss Jessie Starbuck,"

he said, obviously struggling to keep his voice from showing the anger he still felt. "How you come into a place and throw a lot of money around, and upset things in a town. I'll tell you right here and now, I don't intend to let you get away with that, here in Silver City."

"What you've heard and what's true might be two different things," Jessie replied quietly.

"I think I've been around enough to know what's best for my town," Nolan answered.

"And I think you might not know all the truth about the plans your friends have in mind for what you call your town," Jessie told him.

"What do you mean, my friends?"

Jessie could see that her thrusts had upset Nolan. She said levelly, "I don't think I need to explain any further right now. If you don't know what you've gotten into, I suggest that you start finding out."

Nolan started to say something, but thought better of it. He stared at Jessie for a moment, and she could almost feel the hatred that emanated from his pale eyes.

"I see what you're trying to do," he said, spitting out his words like so many bullets. "And it won't work. Now, I've got better things to do than listen to you. Just see that you don't cross me again, Jessie Starbuck. If you do, I'll promise you, you'll be real sorry!"

Nolan turned and strode away before Jessie could reply. She watched him go, a small smile on her face. Ki stepped to her side and stood there until Nolan had disappeared.

"I made myself as inconspicuous as possible," he told her. "Anything I might've done would have been wrong, unless real trouble began, and I was ready for that."

"I understand completely, Ki," Jessie assured him. "You did exactly the right thing. Now let's forget about Nolan and go meet that stage."

"We'd have heard it if it had pulled in," Ki replied. "And

we haven't quite finished our business here yet." He pointed to the old Apache, who had not moved since Jessie threw the *surushin*. "What about him?"

Chapter 7

Jessie looked at the Indian for a moment. He was staring at them, but no expression showed on his deeply wrinkled face. She said, "I think we'd better explain things. I suppose he speaks English; he seemed to understand Nolan's commands without any trouble."

"Let's go talk to him, then," Ki nodded. He ducked through the fence rails, followed by Jessie. They started toward the Apache, and when he saw them moving in his direction he came to meet them.

"Cha-ti-sai thanks you," he told Jessie, in a voice cracked with age. "But why did you help Apache against one of your own?"

"He's not one of our own," Jessie said quickly. "He'd have liked nothing better than to treat us the way he did you."

Cha-ti-sai frowned. "But you owed me nothing, and now I owe you much."

"You don't owe me anything," Jessie said. "And you don't owe the livery stable anything, either. You can take your horse and go home without worrying."

"I do not understand this thing," Cha-ti-sai replied, his eyes searching Jessie's face. "I am of the *Diné*, and your people have no good feeling with us. We have been enemies since your kind first came into our country. Some of our tribes still fight your horse soldiers."

"Is yours one of those tribes?" Ki asked.

Cha-ti-sai shook his head. "No. Not now. But I have led my warriors against your soldiers. I am war chief of Cibique."

"Cibique?" Jessie repeated. "An Apache band?"

"Yes," the old man nodded. "But not like Chiricahua and Jicarilla, we do not still fight. The Black Robes taught us that we could not win. Many of my people went away. There are few left here now."

"Then we can be friends," Jessie said.

"Why do you offer friendship? Who are you, and why are you not like others?"

"My name is Jessie, and this is Ki," Jessie told him. "And don't worry about trying to understand. But if I were you, I'd stay away from Silver City for a while."

Cha-ti-sai nodded slowly. "Yes, this is a true thing. I do not come here much. But I was hungry, and the horse was all I had to sell. It is an old horse, and useless, but it carried me well, into many fights, when I was younger."

"Will you sell it to me?" Jessie asked.

The Apache frowned. "Why would you want a useless horse?"

Jessie was already taking money from her pocket. She found a half eagle and held it out to Cha-ti-sai. "I will pay you now. Here. Take the money."

Cha-ti-sai looked at the five-dollar gold piece and shook his head. "It is too much. A single dollar would even be too much. I have told you, the horse is of no use."

Thinking quickly, Jessie replied, "Only part of it is for the horse. The rest is to pay you for tending to it until I need it, then I'll come and get it from you."

Cha-ti-sai was silent for several moments. Jessie and Ki

could almost feel the intensity of his thoughts. Then he said, "I will attend to your horse well, Jessie."

"Attend to yourself, too," she said. "Use some of that money to buy the food you need. If you aren't well, how can you look after my horse?"

After a moment's thought, the old man nodded. "This is a true thing you say. I will care for your horse well, Jessie. When you want it, come to my village. It is by the tall pines, to the north."

"I'll find it when I'm ready," Jessie promised.

"Then I will take it now and go. The path is long and I do not travel fast."

With a solemn nod, the old Apache turned and walked toward the livery barn. Jessie and Ki watched him until he went into the building, then Ki said, "That was a nice thing to do, Jessie. I don't quite understand why you did it, but I'm sure you had a reason."

"I think I owed him something, Ki. He gave me a chance to open the first wedge between Nolan and the cartel."

"But you made a very big enemy of Nolan," Ki said.

"No bigger than he was even before he saw us the first time, Ki. And I couldn't have planned something that would have given us a chance like this."

Ki shook his head slowly. "I haven't caught up yet."

"Look at it this way," Jessie said. "Nolan's the cartel's man. He'll carry the message back to them that we're ready to fight. Not only that, he's going to do a lot of thinking about what I told him, that he's on the wrong side. It's a gamble, but we've gambled before."

"It does make sense when you put it that way," Ki agreed.

Jessie said, "I want to bring this thing to a head as soon as possible. We'll be better off fighting them in the open than letting them stay in the background."

"I can see that," Ki agreed. "But will we gain enough to pay for the trouble they can cause us?"

"I think so," Jessie answered. "We'll outbid the cartel for locations, and hire men to work the ones we buy. We'll put the geologist to work looking for lodes we can file on ourselves. We'll—" She paused for a moment, frowning thoughtfully.

Ki said, "Those three things will keep us busy, Jessie. Have you thought about how we'll find time to do them with one hand while we fight off the cartel with the other?"

"Oh, I'll admit I haven't worked everything out in sequence yet," Jessie replied. "But I have a feeling that we'll get further by attacking them than by waiting for them to attack us. I may be wrong, but I think it's worth a try. Now let's go around to the hitch rail and wait for the stage."

While Jessie and Ki had already discovered that the stage from Lordsburg to Silver City seldom arrived on schedule, it was later than usual today. The sun hung low over the mountain peaks when the thudding of hooves and the low-pitched growling of wheels on the coarse dirt road brought those who'd been waiting in the building out to the hitch rail. The stage lumbered into sight, moving slowly, one wheel wobbling dangerously. It creaked to a stop as the driver reined in his four-horse team.

"Had a mite of trouble back down the road a ways," he announced to those who stood around the hitch rail. "Wheel come off, and it taken us a little while to jack up the rig and put it back on. Looked for a while like we wasn't going to make it, but we managed to cripple on in."

Jessie and Ki had moved away from the rail when the crowd of waiting men came out of the livery barn. They stood at one side, watching the passengers alighting from the stage. Two women, obviously floozies heading for the cribs, took the carpetbags the driver handed them from the boot and started walking toward the red-lanterned buildings. Then three men wearing rough miners' garb got off, and finally a young man stepped out. He stood beside the stage, inspecting his surroundings in the way any traveler does when arriving at a strange place.

"I think that might be who we're looking for," Jessie said, nudging Ki. "Let's find out."

She and Ki skirted the loosely bunched group inspecting the canted wheel, and started toward the new arrival. He had not seen them yet, but was looking toward the door of the livery. Jessie used the time to take stock of her new employee. He was a young man wearing a felt field-hat. Under a worn corduroy jacket, his wide shoulders indicated a muscular, well-conditioned physique. Turning his head away from the station door, he saw Jessie and Ki moving toward him, and his face showed his relief.

"You'd be Miss Starbuck, I hope?" he asked as they reached him. "I guess you must be, you're the only lady around."

Jessie smiled, extending her hand.

"I'm Clifton Ashmore." As he took her hand briefly, he went on, "Mr. Willard at the First California bank—"

"I know," Jessie interrupted. "We've been looking for you to get here, Mr. Ashmore. And this is Ki. He helps me now, just as he helped my father for many years."

As Ashmore and Ki shook hands, Jessie took stock of the geologist. Besides the powerful build she'd already noted, he had a face tanned to the reddish-bronze hue that many men with fair complexions take on with continued exposure to the outdoors. His hat hid his hair, but the full bristly eyebrows and sideburns showing under it suggested that his hair was blond, as did his blue eyes. Except for the long sideburns, he was clean-shaven. He had full, firm lips and an aggressive jawline.

Turning back to Jessie, Ashmore explained, "I was over in the Comstock Lode country, doing some strata analysis, when Mr. Willard's wire finally got to me. I finished my work and got here just as soon as I could."

"It's a little early for supper, but I'm sure you must be hungry, what with the stage being delayed," Jessie said. "And I know Ki and I are. Suppose we eat now and get better acquainted."

"I'm no hungrier than a snowed-in wolf," Ashmore replied with a smile. "Not that it's the first time. But I'm in favor of your idea, Miss Starbuck."

"We'll leave our horses here, then," she said. "It's not a long walk. When we come back, we'll get you a horse to use while you're here."

"There's a hotel or rooming house where I can find a place to stay, I hope," Ashmore said as they started up Broadway.

"Ki and I are camped up on the ridge above town," Jessie told him. "And I don't think you'd care for the rooming houses here, even if any of them had a room vacant."

"I've seen enough boomtowns to be prepared for that kind of thing, Miss Starbuck," Ashmore said. "So I brought a bedroll just in case I'd need it."

"Jessie and I have been here long enough to learn something about the area," Ki volunteered. "We'll be able to save you a lot of time, looking for locations that seem promising."

"You're just buying locations, then? Not looking for a new lode?" the geologist asked.

"I hope we'll find something new," Jessie replied. "But Ki and I haven't any idea what to look for. We're depending on you to do the prospecting."

"I don't suppose there's an assay office here?"

Ki shook his head. "No, but we've found out that Reynolds's store keeps assay chemicals in stock, for the prospectors who do their own assaying."

"What about borax?" the geologist asked.

"I don't have any idea," Ki replied.

"Neither do I," Jessie added.

"Well, there are some soils that can be used as fluxes, and a few kinds of rock. I'll worry about that later."

"If you'll tell me what you're going to need, chemicals or fluxes or anything else, I'll order them right away," Jessie offered.

"Good," Ashmore said. "But assaying doesn't take a very large amount of anything. I'd imagine I can buy enough from the stores here to do all the assaying you might need."

"I want to start buying proved locations as soon as I can, Mr. Ashmore," Jessie said. "One buying office is already in business, and I'm sure you know that competition for anything in short supply runs prices up."

"Yes, I've seen that everywhere I've been. And by the way, Miss Starbuck, everybody calls me Cliff."

Jessie nodded. "I answer best to Jessie, myself." She pointed to the restaurant sign a short distance ahead. "That place is about as good as any. But I'm sure you know better than to expect anything like the fine restaurants in places like New York or San Francisco."

"I've learned never to expect really civilized eats in a mining boomtown," Ashmore said. "But after that long stagecoach ride, just about any kind of food will satisfy me."

After all three had looked at the menu and settled on venison steak and fried eggs, Ki asked the geologist, "How long will it take you to show Jessie and me how to tell whether a location is worth buying or not?"

"That's a tricky question, Ki," Ashmore said with a smile. "There are times when I have trouble deciding that myself."

"Isn't there some rule of thumb we can go on?" Jessie asked with a tiny frown. "Because either Ki or I will have to look after the office when we open it, while you're out in the field."

"Now, Jessie, even after having met you such a short

time ago, I have an idea that you're pretty good at judging when a man's lying and when he's telling the truth," Ashmore said.

"Most of the time, I can," she replied. Then she added, "I see what you mean, though. If a man has a good location, he'll probably tell the truth about it, and if he's lying, anybody who deals with him should be able to tell."

"Something like that," Ashmore agreed.

"But what about the one who's telling the truth?" Ki asked. "I don't know good silver production from bad."

"Well, until a lode has been proved by a period of production, buying it will be a gamble, whatever you pay. A lode can peter out at any time."

"But if it's been producing for a while, there must be some figures that you start with to calculate what it's worth," Jessie said.

"That depends on whether you're a prospector working by himself on a location he's found, or whether you're thinking in terms of developing a big lode into a large-scale operation," Ashmore answered thoughtfully. "A lone prospector, or one with a partner, can scratch out a living on ore that assays as low as fifteen ounces a ton."

"Fifteen sounds pretty small," Ki commented.

"It is small," the geologist said. "At best, two men can dig and flux enough ore in a week to buy food and maybe a new shirt for one of them."

"What about large-scale mining, then?" Jessie asked.

"There's no trick in figuring that, Jessie. You must average the silver content per ton of ore. Working on a large scale, it costs between fifty and sixty cents to dig and mill a ton of ore and smelt it to produce the pure metal. Silver's pretty well stabilized at a dollar an ounce, so if you have ore yielding more than sixty ounces per ton, you'll be making a good profit."

"What would you call a really rich ore?" Ki asked.

"Oh, anything above a hundred twenty ounces per ton," Ashmore replied. "If you hit a lode that goes more than a hundred fifty, you've got a real bonanza, as long as it holds out."

Jessie said thoughtfully, "I don't suppose there are many that you'd call real bonanzas, though."

"Maybe more than you'd think. All I got on the way up here from Lordsburg was a passing look at the surface conditions, but the soil and topography looked promising in several places that I saw."

"Close to Silver City?" Jessie asked.

"Not very. It was dark before we got near here. But wait until I've had time to look around tomorrow."

"Tell me one more thing," Jessie went on. "Could there be a main lode, what they call a mother lode, around here?"

Ashmore smiled. "There could be such a thing. Virginia City's lode is close to what I'd call one. But if you're hoping to strike a mother lode here, I wouldn't count on it until it's been tested and proved out for a few years."

Before Jessie or Ki could ask any more questions, the waiter arrived with their food. During dinner they had little to say about silver and mining, but chatted at random, getting better acquainted. They returned to the livery stable, rented a horse and saddle for Ashmore, and started for the camp Jessie and Ki had made on the ridge. The sun had set while they were eating, and twilight was merging into darkness. When they drew close to the grove of pines in which they'd pitched their tent, Jessie caught a whiff of an alien odor in the air.

"Do you smell what I do, Ki?" she asked.

"I wondered if I was imagining it," he said. "Somebody in one of those houses we just passed used too much coal oil when they started their supper fire."

"They must've poured with a heavy hand," Ashmore said. "I can smell it too, now."

"Don't worry," Jessie told him. "The wind's low now, but it'll come up a bit later and clear the air."

They rode on in silence for a short distance, then Ki sniffed and said, "I'm not imagining that coal-oil smell now. It's stronger than ever, and I can smell something that's still burning." He looked at Jessie and went on, "Do you have the same idea I'm getting?"

"I'm afraid I do, Ki. Let's speed up."

As they toed their horses to a quicker pace, Ashmore asked, "Is something going on here that you haven't mentioned yet?"

"There's not much going on yet, but there will be later, Cliff. I didn't mention it during dinner; I wanted to save it until we were in a more private place. But—" she broke off as Ki spoke.

"My hunch was right, Jessie, but it came too late. And so did we, I'm afraid. Look."

Jessie looked at the pine grove. There was no sign of their tent or bedding. Instead, on the spot where the tent had stood there was a black area of charred ground, and the smell of kerosene mixed with freshly burned cloth hung heavily in the air.

"You mean someone's burned your tent and gear?" Ashmore exclaimed incredulously. "Who'd do a thing like that? There's an unwritten law around mining camps that nobody damages anything useful, like a bedroll or tent. They're too hard to replace."

"I'm positive who did it," Jessie said. "And I'm sure Ki is, too."

"Nolan, of course," Ki said unhesitatingly. "Or one of his men. He'd have someone to handle jobs like this, of course."

"Who is Nolan?" Ashmore asked.

"He's the town marshal," Jessie replied. "We had a little

run-in earlier today, and I'm sure this is his way of getting back at us."

Before Ashmore could ask any further questions, they'd reached the burned area. A few tiny wisps of oily smoke still rose from the scraps of burned bedding and canvas.

"I wish there was another hour of light!" Ki exclaimed. He pointed to a faint depression in the ground at the edge of the burned spot. Looking closely, Jessie saw the faint print of a boot heel with two protruding nails. Ki went on, "In another few minutes it'll be too dark for me to follow a trail, even one as clear as this one."

"From what you're saying, I gather there's someone in Silver City who doesn't feel exactly friendly toward you, Jessie," Ashmore remarked. "Perhaps you'd better tell me about it, so I'll know what to be on the lookout for."

"I mentioned earlier that I wanted to explain the situation to you," Jessie told him. "And I'll do it just as soon as Ki and I look around before it's dark, to make sure that whoever set the fire didn't leave a few surprise traps scattered around."

"Traps?" Ashmore asked, raising his eyebrows in surprise.

"Things like set-guns or a buried bear trap," Ki replied. "Jessie's right, Cliff. Explanations can come later."

"You might not like what you'll hear," Jessie added. "But if you decide after I've told you that you don't want to stay, I'll understand."

"You don't know me very well yet, Jessie," Ashmore said. "I took this job because it interested me, and I've never yet turned my back on a job that was dangerous. Unless what you're doing is illegal, you've hired me, and I'll stay with you till the job's finished, no matter what happens!"

Chapter 8

"How's the location-buying business, Jessie?" Ashmore asked as he came into the tent early in the afternoon and dropped his knapsack on the ground with a thud.

"It's been very good today," she replied, looking behind him in anticipation of seeing Ki come in. After a moment she realized the geologist was alone, and asked, "Did Ki go straight to camp instead of stopping by?"

"No, he stayed at the new location for a while. He's doing the hard part of my job for me, trying to find out how big the carbonate formation is. He said he'd be there for supper, though."

"You're going up to camp, then?"

"Yes. There are some assays I want to do before dark."

"I think I'll just close up shop and go with you," Jessie said. "I outbid Mineral Developments for three more locations today, and I can afford to let them have any more that I might miss out on by leaving early."

A friendship had developed quickly between Jessie and the young geologist, though they'd been together very little of the time since his arrival. For the first two weeks, Ashmore had spent the daylight hours learning the country around

Silver City, visiting the small mines that dotted the area, and since then had been trying to find new locations on which Jessie could file.

Jessie's attentions had been concentrated on getting her location-buying office set up. The day after the camp-burning, Ki had made a hurried trip to Lordsburg and returned with two tents. One was a large wall tent that would accommodate all three of them on nights when rain or the cold thin fog that sometimes wisped across the high peaks and ridges made sleeping in the open either impossible or uncomfortable.

He'd also bought a smaller tent that they'd squeezed into a narrow space between two stores, almost directly across Broadway from the office of the cartel's buyer. Shortly after the camp had been made habitable again and the tent set up on Broadway, Ashmore had asked Ki to give him a hand in exploring an area where he'd found an interesting formation. Ki and the geologist had begun leaving early and returning late, and Jessie had seen little of them for several days.

She'd spent all her time in the buying office. Strangely, she'd noticed no open reaction from the cartel-operated Mineral Developments office across the street. As the days passed, Jessie decided that the cartel's local operator must either be plotting some kind of action that took time to bring off, or was ignoring her competition while he waited for instructions from the cartel's bosses.

Tate Nolan had also kept out of sight. Jessie had seen the town marshal only once, swaggering down Broadway during the early afternoon. While she'd welcomed the apparent peace, which had allowed her to give full time to the new location-buying effort, she had an uncomfortable feeling that it might be just the calm that came before a storm.

As they mounted their horses and started riding up Broadway, Jessie told Ashmore, "Those three locations I bought today make eight I've taken away from Mineral Developments this week."

"That fellow running the place across the street ought to be really upset by now," Ashmore said.

"I certainly won't be unhappy if he is," she said, then went on with a frown, "It's odd, though. I still haven't seen him. He must go in and out by the back door, but if he's trying to avoid me, he's wasting his time. I'm not at all interested in getting acquainted with him."

"You're certainly encouraging him to be angry, the way you've taken locations away from him."

"Oh, he doesn't need any encouragement to be angry with me, Cliff," Jessie replied as they reached the end of Broadway and turned off the road onto the trail that mounted the ridge.

"It seems to me he'd be upset because you've been outbidding him on the good locations."

"I'd think so too," she agreed. "Especially since the outfit he's working for is owned by a bigger firm that's been competing with the Starbuck enterprises for years."

Jessie had revealed to Ashmore only part of the reason for her interest in competing for silver locations with the British-owned cartel front. In her explanation she had not mentioned the cartel, or the sinister criminal side of its international conspiracy. All that Jessie had told him was that the purpose of her presence in Silver City was to keep a European firm from getting a stranglehold on the mines in that mineral-rich area of New Mexico.

Ashmore said, "You might not want to bother with a lot of small locations anymore, after I've assayed the samples that I've brought back and the ones that Ki will be coming in with later this afternoon."

"That's the location you and Ki have been working on for the past three or four days?"

Ashmore nodded. "We're still in the same place, about

two miles off the old military road that runs from the abandoned fort west of Pinos Altos."

"Have you found something really good?"

"It's too early to say. When I left, Ki was still pegging away with a star drill, trying to find out how large an area the lode covers. But it looks like you've filed on a really rich location."

"How rich?"

"That'll depend on how big the lode is, and how the samples I've brought back show up when I run my assay."

One of the first things Ashmore had done when they set up camp had been to build one of the little beehive-shaped adobe ovens that he could use for making sample assays. The process was not a complicated one, and he assured them that his findings were almost as accurate as those he'd have made using more elaborate equipment.

They came to the crest of the ridge and followed it to their camp. It stood apart from the nearest houses, which had been built as close as possible to the creek that trickled down the slope toward the town. To provide them with fresh water, Ki and Ashmore had dug a narrow ditch to camp from the spring out of which the creek rose just below the crest.

As they swung off their horses, the geologist said, "I'm going to build a fire in the oven before I unsaddle my horse. I'm very curious about those ore samples."

"Go ahead and start work," Jessie said. "It's no more trouble to take off two saddles than one. I'll come watch you when I take care of them and wash up."

By the time Jessie went to the oven, Ashmore had three of the samples ready. He'd already crushed the carbonate in the mortar he carried in his field kit, and divided the powder into three parts. The samples stood on the ground beside the oven in small, deep bowls of thick porcelain a bit larger than a teacup, each filled to about one-third of its capacity with a carefully measured amount of the sandlike, silver-bearing carbonate.

Jessie had seen Ashmore perform assays before, but the process continued to fascinate her. She watched him sprinkle the surface of the carbonate with charcoal, stir the fine black powder into it, and put each cup into the oven with a pair of tongs. Finally he leaned a tin plate over the opening to create a concentrated draft, and stood up.

"We'll know how good your new location is about two hours from now," he said, picking up a pail that stood close by.

"If you're going to the spring, Cliff, I'll walk along with you," she volunteered. "The water's so cold and clear, I always enjoy a drink from it. It's certainly not like the water that comes out of the town pump."

They reached the spring, a bubbling stream that spurted out of a huge split in a low wall of stone and bubbled into a sizable pool of clear shimmering water. Ashmore set the bucket down beside the pool, and as Jessie started to kneel, he took her hand and held it while she lowered herself to her knees. He held it a moment or two longer than was really necessary. Jessie glanced up at him and smiled her thanks before she dipped her cupped palm into the cold water and drank.

Ashmore dropped to his knees beside her and braced his palms on the ground, then leaned forward and drank directly from the spring. As he straightened his arms to push himself up, one hand slipped on the moist earth and into the pool. He tried to stop himself from falling, but was too badly off balance. Jessie reached out to help him, but she too was on her knees, and her balance was as precarious as his.

She felt herself being pulled into the water by Ashmore's weight, but was unable to straighten up. Ashmore's hand reached the bottom of the pool and stopped his fall, but by now Jessie was in the water as well. Her arms, shorter than his, did not touch bottom, and Ashmore wrapped his free arm around her just in time to keep her from plunging completely into the pool.

They knelt beside the little pond, Ashmore's arm still holding Jessie, water running from their hair and dripping from their chins. Only half of Ashmore's shirt had gotten wet, but Jessie's soaked blouse was clinging to her, and her high firm breasts stood out boldly, their nipples taut and showing clearly through the wet cloth. Jessie saw Ashmore's wry smile fade as his eyes widened. Then he pulled her to him and his lips sought hers.

In spite of her surprise, Jessie responded at first, then broke off their kiss as Ashmore's tongue touched her lips. She pulled away, and he released her readily. They knelt facing one another for a moment without speaking.

"I'm sorry, Jessie," Ashmore said. "I didn't think before I grabbed you. It's not exactly good manners for a fellow to kiss his boss unless he knows she wants him to."

"You don't need to apologize, Cliff," she replied. "There might be times when a boss wants to be kissed, and shows it without realizing what she's doing."

"You're not angry, then?"

"No. Surprised, but—well, I don't think there's a woman alive who isn't flattered when a good-looking man kisses her."

"I'm glad you're not mad." He smiled sheepishly. "I was stupid to give way to an impulse like that."

Always honest with herself, Jessie faced the fact that she'd enjoyed the kiss. "I don't think you were stupid, Cliff," she replied. "In fact, if this place wasn't so public, with somebody from one of those houses down the slope apt to come up here anytime, I'd be tempted to invite you to kiss me again."

His eyes lighting up, the young geologist stammered, "You—you really mean that?"

"Even though we haven't been together long, you should have learned by now that I don't say anything I don't mean." Jessie stood up and ran her hands over her mane of tawny-gold hair to stop the dripping water that was still running from it. "But you'll have to wait for the next kiss, Cliff. Fill the bucket, and let's go back to camp."

They walked side by side, Cliff carefully keeping his distance until Jessie linked her arm in his and pulled him closer to her. He looked down at her, his gaze a mixture of admiration and puzzlement. She returned his look with a smile, but did not offer her lips to him. When they reached the tent, Jessie said, "Do your assay samples need any attention, Cliff?"

"Not now. The amalgamation will take another hour."

"Then we don't need to wait, do we?" she asked, leading him into the tent.

For a moment after the flaps had fallen into place behind them, Ashmore stood motionless. Then he swept Jessie into his arms and crushed her to him while his lips found hers. This time she did not reject his questing tongue, but met it with her own, and they stood in their embrace until both were breathless.

As they reluctantly parted, Jessie began unbuttoning Cliff's wet shirt. For a moment he stood quietly, then as her fingers brushed his chest repeatedly, he reached for Jessie's blouse and pulled it free of her belt. His hands crept under the soft moist fabric, warm on Jessie's skin. She reached the last button of his shirt and worked it off his shoulders, revealing a broad chest with almost boyishly soft skin, broken by a vee of short, fine, reddish-brown curls.

Cliff's hands had found Jessie's breasts by now, and were cupping their soft firmness. Jessie offered her lips again, and he met them with his. They stood swaying in the center of the dim light that filtered through the canvas, while Jessie's hands slid down Cliff's waist to his belt.

Unbuckling it, she quickly flicked open his fly and slid her hand inside, finding him swollen and throbbing as she closed her fingers around his shaft.

She stopped their kiss slowly and gently to whisper, "Hurry and finish undressing, Cliff, while I get my clothes off."

Curling up to sit on her bedroll, which took up the rear part of the tent, Jessie levered off her boots and slipped off her jeans. She pushed the discarded clothing aside and stood up. Cliff's eyes had not left her. He was gazing in admiration at her firm, lithe body, breasts standing proudly above her slim waist, which tapered into the rounded swell of her hips, where a gleaming triangle of golden fleece was centered at the beginning of her slim but fully rounded thighs.

"You're a beautiful woman, Jessie," Cliff breathed. "I've tried ever since the minute I first saw you to imagine what you'd look like this way, but my imagination was a lot short of what I'm looking at now."

Wordlessly, Jessie stood and went to him. Her movement broke the spell that watching her had cast over him. He kicked off his calf-high boots, and began pushing down his jeans. Jessie was beside him by now. She put her hands beside his and helped him pull his jeans away, then stepped in front of him.

Grasping his erection, she stroked its rounded length softly with her fingertips before pressing herself close to him, feeling him throb as she clasped his burning, fleshy cylinder between the warm softness of her thighs. Cliff bent to kiss her again, and Jessie deftly turned the move into a backward step that placed them at the edge of her bedding. She stopped there to let their lips meet once again, and as their kiss deepened and intensified, she let her muscles relax slowly until the weight of her body drew him down with her to the outspread blankets.

Cliff rose above her, and Jessie guided him between her

outspread thighs until she felt him sinking into her, filling her. She clasped her legs tightly around his hips as he began stroking, slowly at first, then almost imperceptibly faster, until his thrusts became fierce lunges.

Giving herself up to her mounting feelings, Jessie rolled beneath him, raising her body in time to his rhythm, lost now in a world of sensation that mounted until she wrapped her arms around his waist and pulled him to her, forcing him to stop his motion.

"What's wrong, Jessie?" he gasped. "I'm—"

"Nothing's wrong," she said. "But we don't need to be in a hurry. Lie quietly for a few minutes now. We'll enjoy each other all the more if we aren't in a rush."

"But I—" Cliff began.

Jessie stopped his words with her lips, and while they lay motionless, their flicking tongues entwining in mouth-to-mouth caresses, she began using her inner muscles, as she'd been taught by the wise old geisha to whom Alex had entrusted her sexual education at the proper time of her development into mature womanhood.

Cliff gasped when he felt himself grasped by Jessie's gently vibrating muscles. She continued her caresses until she felt his body grow taut, then she relaxed and simply held him in place with her encircling arms until he'd grown quiescent again.

"Now," she whispered to him. "Now."

Seeking her lips with his once more, Cliff moved. He raised himself slowly at first and sank into her gently and deeply. Then both of them were caught up in the timeless rhythm, and he thrust harder and faster and Jessie matched his movements until they were lost in one another, mounting to the ultimate sensation that lifted them and swept over them like a great billowing wave, until Cliff gasped and Jessie cried out with joy.

She fell back, pulling her lover with her, feeling the

pulsations that shook him in tempo with her fading shudders until all feeling ebbed and they lay quietly contented.

"You're a very satisfying lover, Cliff," Jessie whispered in his ear as his head lay on her shoulder.

He turned to kiss her neck and cheek, and replied, "You're amazing, Jessie. I—well, I can't find the right words to tell you, but I hope you understand what I'm trying to say."

"I think I do," she told him. "Now let's just lie quietly and rest for a moment. I hate to bring the world back to us, but there are things waiting to be done, and we'll have other times to be together."

"I know you're right," he said reluctantly. "But I don't want to let you go."

"And I don't want you to," she assured him. "But both of us know we must."

Slowly Cliff released her. They rose and dressed silently in the dimness of the tent. Cliff went outside first, and after a few moments Jessie came out and found him gazing at the little adobe oven, transparent waves of heat shimmering above it in the clear air of the waning afternoon.

"Leaving your ore samples in the oven such a long time didn't ruin your assay, did it?" Jessie asked.

"No. Usually I'd have taken them out before now, but timing's not critical in making fusion assays."

Cliff moved to the oven and picked up the tongs, lifted the porcelain crucibles out one by one, and placed them on the tin that he'd used as an oven door. Jessie looked into the small white containers. The concentrate was inky black now, and as she watched it, the smooth, fluid surface began to change texture and grow rough and mottled.

"In a few minutes I can turn it out of the crucibles," Cliff said. "Then it'll cool very fast."

They watched the little domes as they grew, lost their sheen, and changed and contracted until they were rough, misshapen black lumps. Cliff brought the pail of water to the oven, picked up the lumps, and dropped them in. The water began bubbling, and steam rose from its surface. Jessie's anticipation mounted to impatience as she waited. At last Cliff took the lumps out of the bucket and picked up his miner's hammer.

"We won't know the whole story for a while longer," he told Jessie, bringing the hammer down on the nearest chunk. "But we can get an idea of what we might have."

Another blow was needed to crack the lump. It fell apart, and among the small black chunks left when it shattered, Jessie saw a roughly shaped globule of a lighter color.

"Is that silver?" she asked.

"Only part of it," he replied. "It'll take a while longer to find out how much."

He dropped the globule into the pail and broke the other lumps, dropping the globules that had formed in their centers into the pail with the first. Plunging his hand into the pail, he found the first globule by feel and lifted it out. It glistened wetly for only a moment before its sheen faded and he held a slightly misshapen gray ball in his fingers.

"Silver?" Jessie asked.

"No." Cliff shook his head as he turned the ball. "There's silver in it, but there's also some lead and a bit of copper, and if it's like most unrefined silver, quite probably a trace of gold as well."

"But does it look good or bad?" she persisted.

"I'm almost afraid to answer you, Jessie," Cliff said. "I don't remember many assays when I've recovered a button this big. Even allowing for the other metals, this looks like it's going to be one of the richest silver ores I've ever seen. This might just be that mother lode you asked me about!"

Chapter 9

For a moment after Cliff had made his unexpected revelation, Jessie sat silent. She was thinking of more riches being added to the great wealth of the Starbuck holdings, and it struck her as unfair somehow that the location on which she'd filed should contain such a huge store of potential worth. There were, she thought, hundreds of prospectors with little except a few dollars, determination, and the will to keep going, who deserved to have made the discovery far more than she did.

Then she looked at the opposite side of the coin, and was thankful that she had been the one to file on the location, rather than a prospector who might have sold his rights to the cartel. Such a sale would have increased a thousandfold that sinister organization's capacity to do evil.

Jessie's introspection lasted but a few seconds. Finally she asked, "How long will it take you to find out how rich the ore really is?"

"Not long. All that I have left to do is cupel this button and weigh the *doré* bead. Then I'll reduce it and weigh it again, and we'll know."

"I don't know what you mean by 'cupel,'" she told Cliff. "But go ahead and do it. I can see you want to know, and I'll admit that I'm as curious as you are."

"'Cupel' is just an assay term," Cliff explained. "It's a way to take the lead and other impurities out of the button."

While he was speaking, Cliff had taken a small, shallow, saucerlike dish of reddish clay from his kitbag and laid the button on it. Reaching back in the bag, he brought out a pinch of pinhead-sized gray pellets and let them trickle over the button, then placed the saucer in the tongs and set it carefully on the bed of coals that still remained in the oven.

"Those little lead pellets will melt fast," he explained. "The button will melt a little bit more slowly, and when it does, the lead and other impurities in it will combine with what's already melted. The fluid metal will seep into the clay, and the silver left in the dish will be the *doré* bead, which is what's really measured."

"What about the gold?" Jessie asked. "Surely you don't call that an impurity, do you?"

"No. It stays in the bead, but I'll separate it from the silver later."

Jessie and the geologist sat on their heels in front of the open door, watching the lead pellets melt, and finally the button itself began to shine with a bright silvery sheen and started to shrink. When the button vanished, Cliff quickly took the dish out with the tongs and rotated it expertly. The bottom of the cupel now turned bright as it absorbed the molten lead. Cliff kept rotating the dish until a button or bead formed in the bottom. It was much smaller than the original button, and also much brighter.

Cliff dipped his hand in the pail of water and sprinkled the dish. The lead that coated the bottom began to grow duller than the bead remaining in its center. With a quick darting move born of long practice, Cliff picked up the bead with his still-wet thumb and forefinger and rolled it in the palm of his hand for a few moments. He handed the bead to Jessie.

"That's the *doré* bead," he said. "Hold on to it for a minute, while I get my scales."

Jessie looked at the little bead that glistened in the palm of her hand. It was a bit lopsided, and still quite warm. It was also heavier than she'd thought it would be, for it was only as large in diameter as the tip of her thumb.

Meanwhile, Cliff had set up his field balance. He made precise adjustments of the balance-lever until the indicator arrow stood at zero, then motioned to Jessie to place the bead in the sample pan. The arrow moved a fraction of an inch and wobbled for a few seconds before stopping. He noted the weight on a pad from the kit, and put the pad aside.

Taking a whiskey shotglass and a thick, glass-stoppered bottle from the kit, he dropped the *doré* bead in the glass and poured in enough of the liquid from the bottle to cover it. He swirled the glass and a thin vapor rose, bringing to Jessie's nose a sharp, acrid smell.

She had watched Cliff's deft movements with interest, but without understanding. Now she asked, "Can you tell me what's happening without going into a lot of mysterious details and using terms I don't understand?"

"Oh, sure. The *doré* button had both silver and gold in it when I weighed it after it was cupeled. Now I'm dissolving the silver with nitric acid, which doesn't have any effect on gold. In a minute I'll weigh the gold that will be left in the glass, and subtract that from the weight of the button. That'll give me the silver content of the button. Since I know how much the ore samples weighed, it's just a matter of simple multiplication to figure out how much silver there is in a ton of ore."

"You can tell that from the tiny little bit of ore you started with?"

"Sure. Like I said, it's just simple arithmetic."

Cliff looked at the glass. The vapor had stopped rising now, and in the bottom of the glass there was a speck of gold the size of a pinhead. He carefully poured off the acid and lowered the glass into the water bucket until it was half-filled.

After swirling the water, the speck of gold almost invisible in it, he emptied the water out and washed the glass and its tiny blob of gold again. Then he lowered his finger into the glass and pushed its tip down on the bit of gold.

Holding the speck of precious metal very carefully, he moved his hand over the scale and dropped the gold into the balance pan. This time, determining the precise weight of the metal took several moments. When the pointer was finally centered, Cliff jotted down its weight and began scribbling figures rapidly, while Jessie watched with mounting impatience. At last he looked up, his eyebrows raised.

"Well?" Jessie asked. "Is the figure good, or bad?"

"I'll want to check it by running those other two samples, Jessie," he replied. "But unless I'm wrong, you've got a very, very rich lode of silver in that location."

"How rich is very, very rich?" she asked.

"Over four hundred ounces to the ton. Of course, it may just be a small lode; we'll have to wait until Ki gets back to find that out. But even if it's small, it's worth working. And there'll be a little bit of gold, and perhaps some platinum and copper, that smelting will bring out of the silver."

Jessie whistled softly under her breath. In the short time she'd had the location-buying office in operation, the richest one she'd been offered had assayed one hundred eighty ounces per ton. Most of the locations had ranged from sixty to one hundred twenty ounces; ore with less than sixty ounces was not profitable to mine.

"I can't just let it stay in the ground," she said. "Not even if the lode's a small one."

"We'll know its size in a few days, after we find out how much area the formation covers. If you're thinking about working it, though, there are a few catches."

"What are they, Cliff?"

"There's the dirt overlay, a stratum of limestone, another of slate, and then still another stratum of limestone above the ore vein. Under it, there's more limestone. Developing a lode like that will be expensive and will take a lot of men."

"That doesn't sound any worse than the Comstock," Jessie said, frowning thoughtfully. "The diggings there are pretty deep."

"Yes, of course. So are some other big producers. But I'd suggest you do some exploration first."

"What kind of exploration?"

"Put down a small shaft or two. Even that will cost quite a bit. You'll have to put in a small stamping mill and reduction equipment. That means buildings and machinery. And for the mine itself, you'll need men and a lot of lumber and shoring timbers."

"And we're a long way from the railroad," Jessie added. "So it'll cost more to ship the ore to a smelter."

"Exactly," Ashmore agreed.

"Even that doesn't bother me, Cliff," she said. "I've learned a little bit about mining. There are some copper mines up in Montana that father developed. I've been up there and gone through them a time or two, so I know pretty well what you're talking about."

"This isn't something you can decide now, Jessie. I think your best bet is to put down a small shaft or two. There are always a few prospectors at loose ends in town here."

"Oh, I could probably hire every man who came in the office with a location to sell," Jessie told him. "After they've sold, I'm sure a lot of them would probably be glad to get a steady job long enough to build up a grubstake."

"You might want to hire some help later," Ashmore went on. "But my guess right now is that the entire lode will turn out to be soft concentrate. You can reduce it in a roller trough, and if we hit too much rock later, I can build a little stamping mill. It won't be fancy, but it'll handle all the ore we'd take out of a couple of small exploratory shafts."

"Even those are going to need boards and shoring timbers," she said, thinking aloud. "And Tate Nolan seems to have a monopoly on the lumber that comes into town. He won't sell to me, of course."

"There's plenty of standing timber," Ashmore said. "We can hire a few men to cut enough for the exploratory shafts."

"Yes, I was just thinking the same thing," Jessie said. "But there are some other things I've got to take care of before I can think about starting a silver mine."

"Well, you don't have to decide right now. But when Ki gets back to camp and we go in for supper, I'm going to buy the best bottle of champagne I can find in Silver City, and we'll toast your good luck."

"I feel like celebrating now," Jessie told him. "And it's not likely Ki will get back before dark. Come on, Cliff. Let's go back into the tent."

Ki had lost track of the number of exploratory holes he'd put down since Cliff Ashmore had left to assay the samples taken from the face of the silver lode. With a glance at the low-hanging sun, he dropped his sledgehammer, straightened up, and hauled the long shaft of the star drill out of the hole he'd just put down. Wiping the end of his touch-pole, he smeared it with a bit of fresh pitch, then lowered it down the hole. When he pulled it out again, particles of dull, dun-colored, sandy ore instead of chips of white limestone were clinging to the pitch. The particles told Ki that the hole he'd just drilled was still over the lode.

This was the routine he'd been going through most of

the day, as he and Ashmore tried to find the extent of the lode on the new location. While the geologist dug into the face of the cliff and took samples for assaying, Ki had begun trying to find out the extent of the silver-bearing carbonate sands.

Ki had learned enough, from Ashmore and from experience, to know what he was doing. The ore vein, or lode, was typical of that area. The carbonate, silver-bearing ore, formed a thick layer between two layers of limestone, like the icing between two layers of cake.

In this particular location, a layer of slate was just below a thin surface covering of dirt, the upper limestone formation below the slate. By drilling a series of holes spaced fifteen to twenty feet apart, deep enough to reach the relatively soft ore, it was possible to determine the extent of the underground lode.

Laying the touch-pole aside, Ki decided he'd covered all the ground possible for the day. He gathered up his tools and started for the twin pines that he and Ashmore used as hitching posts. The trees stood a few paces beyond the dropoff of the low ledge through which he'd been drilling.

Ki tossed the tools to the ground before leaping down. He put his hammer and star drills and the touch-pole at the base of the ledge and scraped loose pebbles over them, though nothing had been disturbed at the location since he and Ashmore had started working it.

Going to his horse, Ki sipped from the canteen that hung from a saddlestring and shook a bit more limestone dust off his loose-fitting trousers and jacket. Swinging into the saddle, he started the ride back to Silver City. He'd covered most of the way to town when he saw the still form lying at the edge of the rutted dirt road ahead.

Scanning the thin growth of scrub pines that stretched from each side of the road, he saw that no ambush was possible in that sparsely wooded area. When he reached the prone man, Ki reined in and dismounted.

He put a hand on the back of the sprawled-out man and felt a strong, steady heartbeat. Turning him over, Ki saw that the only indication of what had happened was a red, swollen weal on the man's forehead. Stepping to the horse, he returned with the canteen and sprinkled water on the man's face.

While he continued his ministrations, Ki studied the face of the unconscious man. He was probably in his late fifties or early sixties, judging by his wrinkles and by the stubble of white beard that covered his chin. His face was streaked with road grime, but the water Ki continued sprinkling soon washed away most of the layer of dust. After a few minutes more had passed, the man opened his eyes and looked up.

"Who in hell are you?" he asked.

"Never mind about that right now," Ki replied. "How do you feel?"

"Like you would, if some dirty sonofabitchin' robber had slammed you on the head with the barrel of his pistol."

"You were held up? Robbed?"

"Sure I was, boy. You don't think I'd lay down for a nap right alongside the road, do you?"

"Of course not," Ki replied. "How many robbers were there, and what did they take?"

"They was three of 'em, I'm purty shore. I only got a good look at one, and he had on a bandanna that covered his face up to his eyes."

"How do you know there were more, then?" Ki frowned.

"Well, I seen this one feller settin' his horse in the middle of the road, and started to rein in. About the time I got near enough to see he had a bandanna around his face, he throwed down on me with a double-barrel shotgun."

"You didn't see his face, either, then?"

"Not a glimmer. Then I heard somebody climbing up on the wagon in back of me, and scrabbling over my load. He dropped down on the seat by me, and all I really seen of him was a Colt pistol. He swung the barrel down on my head, and that's all I knowed till you begun putting water on my face."

"What about the third man?"

"I'm jest right shore I heard another one jump up on the load about the time the one that hit me swung his gun down."

"You didn't get a look at their horses, then?" Ki asked, adding quickly, "Except for the one the man in the road was riding?"

"Not a glimmer. He was forkin' a right pretty chestnut gelding, though. It might've been branded, but I don't know. I guess it was my fault, not payin' mind to things."

"You couldn't have done anything, if he had you covered," Ki pointed out. "I don't guess you carry a gun?"

"Not unless it's my huntin' rifle, when I go out for a deer to keep the pot boilin'. But I shore wisht I'd had it this trip. It cost me a pretty penny, the lumber and my horse and wagon to boot. That's just about all I got in the world."

"You've had a heavy loss," Ki agreed. "But we'll talk about the robbers later, and see if you can remember anything more about them. Do you feel like you can ride the rump of my horse into Silver City?"

"I reckon. It wouldn't be the first time I rid that way." He cocked his head and looked at Ki curiously, then asked, "You got a name, ain't you?"

"Yes. It's Ki."

"Ki what?"

"It's the only name I use. And I guess I'd better ask your name, too, now that I'm sure you're not hurt badly."

"Name's Jenkins. Zeb Jenkins. Short for Zebulon. My folks always did admire General Pike."

"Let's get you on the horse and get started, then. There's not much we can do until we get to town."

Ki started slowly down the road; then, after he was sure

that Zeb Jenkins was able to keep his balance, he toed the horse into a faster walk. Over his shoulder he asked, "What kind of load were you hauling, Zeb?"

"A big load of pine boards. Taken me the better part of a week to whipsaw, too."

"And you were going to sell them in Silver City?"

"I shore was aimin' to. Feller passin' by my cabin the other day, he said folks was needin' a lot of lumber there right now."

"Well, that's true enough," Ki said. "But you didn't have a buyer waiting for them?"

"A'course not! How could I of? I just finished sawin' 'em last night."

"Just curious," Ki said. "Well, when we get to Silver City, I'll see if I can help you find your wagon and load."

"Why?" Zeb asked. "You don't know me from Adam's off-ox, and you sure don't owe me no more favors."

"I don't look on it as a favor," Ki said. "If I was in your situation, I'd like for somebody to help me."

"Damned if you don't talk like a good Christian white man instead of a heathen Chinee!" the old man exclaimed.

"I happen to be Japanese," Ki told him. "And even if I don't pray to your god, neither my people nor the Chinese are heathens. Our religions are older than yours."

"Well, that may be—" the old man began, then he thought better of what he was about to say and closed his mouth.

Ki went on as though the other hadn't spoken. He asked, "Did anybody but your family know you were going to be hauling that load of lumber to Silver City today?"

"Nobody knowed but me and Wanda. Hell, Ki, I didn't know myself until late last night, when I got my last planks cut and finished loading my wagon."

"Wanda's your wife, I suppose?"

"You're supposin' wrong," Zeb replied. "She's my little girl. Elvira—she was my wife, but she up and died."

Ki nodded and repeated his question. "And you hadn't told anybody in Silver City when you'd be bringing your load in?"

"Nope. Nary a soul."

"Did you tell any of your neighbors about your plans?"

"Shee-it!" Zeb exclaimed. "I didn't have t' tell 'em. They nosed around my cabin and found out, soon as I begun fellin' the pines. None of 'em didn't offer to help none, but they'd come gawk at me when I was doing my whipsawin'."

"You run a sawmill, then?" Ki asked.

"Hell no, Ki! I ain't in the lumber business. I do jest what cuttin' and board-makin' I need to keep me and Wanda in grub while I go prospectin' when I'm in between locations. When I find a good lode, I work it till it gives out, then go lookin' for the next one."

Ki nodded, satisfied now that whoever had robbed Zeb could not have planned the theft in advance. Mulling over the robbery as they jogged along toward Silver City, he decided quickly that his best course would be to take Zeb to their camp, and get Jessie's ideas about how far she'd want him to go in helping the old man. He said nothing to Zeb about his plan, but when they reached the edge of town he turned his horse up the slope and started toward the ridge.

"Hey, hold on, Ki!" Zeb protested. "You said you was gonna take me to town!"

"I will, Zeb. But I've got to let my boss know I'm back, and see if she has anything else for me to do before we go in."

"You work for somebody, then?"

"I work for a lady named Jessie Starbuck."

"Well," Zeb said, "I was a mite curious about what a Chi—I mean Japanese man like you was doin' around here, but I didn't wanta pry. This Miz Starbuck, she a rich widow, seein' as how she can afford to hire a servant?"

"Jessie's no widow. She's a young lady, and I worked

for her father before he died, so I stayed to help her."

"It all sinks in now, I guess," Zeb said. "I wouldn't want to get a man that's helped me in trouble with his boss, and I know lady bosses is likely t' git pritty persnickety. Take your time, Ki. I ain't got no load of lumber to haul, and I don't guess it's likely I will have anytime soon, so it don't much matter what we do right now."

Ki knew that nothing he could say would cheer Zeb up. He did not reply, and the old man matched his silence as the horse plodded up the slope toward the camp.

Chapter 10

"I'll agree with you that it was probably some of Nolan's men who stole Zeb's lumber and wagon, Ki," Jessie said after she and Cliff had listened to Zeb's story and Ki's account of finding him unconscious beside the road. "But I don't see how we can do much about getting it back."

"Hiding a horse and a wagon loaded with lumber can't be the easiest thing in the world, Jessie," Cliff Ashmore pointed out. "Especially in a little place like Silver City."

"It's like I told Zeb," Ki put in. "The thieves probably hid the wagon up some little canyon, and won't bring it into town until it's dark."

"Either that or they delivered it to a mine that they knew would buy shoring lumber, and unloaded it there," Ashmore said. "I know how desperate a mine operator gets when he can't push a shaft ahead for lack of timbers. They'd buy lumber from anybody who offered them some, and ask no questions."

"In that case, we'd never have a chance to find it," Jessie said. "There are dozens of locations being worked around here."

When Ki and Zeb had reached camp, Ashmore was there

alone, just finishing his sampling. The three men had gone to town at once, where they'd found Jessie still at the tent on Broadway. Ki and Zeb had joined in telling her about the robbery, and her reaction had been just what Ki had foreseen it would be.

Zeb had been listening to the others without speaking. Now he said, "I ain't tryin' to tell you folks how to go about things, but was it me, I'd go palaver with this Nolan feller, even if he is the town lawman. But I sure wouldn't go without I had a gun in my hand ready to let him have it if he lied."

"We don't have anything at all to accuse Nolan of," Jessie said. "I'm sorry as anybody can be about your loss, Zeb, but it's impossible to identify a load of lumber. One board looks just like another."

"Beg your pardon, Miz Jessie, but that ain't so. Leastwise, not in this case."

"What do you mean?" Jessie frowned.

"I mean ever' one of them boards has got my mark on it. You see, when I was sawin' boards back in Kaintucky, the feller I worked for had three or four of us on the job, and he paid us by the board. So all of us had t' mark the ones we cut. I got into the habit, and I ain't ever lost it."

"Your lumber was marked, then?" Jessie asked. "How?"

"Same way I always mark my boards," Zeb replied. "When one of my rifle shell cases gits so wore around the primer hold that it ain't no good no more, I save it, 'cause the bullet end's still got sharp edges. And I tap four circles with them shells on one butt-end or ever' board I cut."

"But that only lasts until someone saws off the end of the board," Ashmore objected. "Then your boards would be just like any others."

"Now, that ain't perzactly right," Zeb told the geologist. "Far's I know, I'm the only one hereabouts that makes boards with a whipsaw. There ain't too many good whipsaw hands left no more. Ever'body that makes lumber now uses a two-man bucksaw, or one of them newfangled treadle mills with a blade as big around as my arm's long and a mule or horse to work the treadle."

"I don't see what difference that makes," Jessie said.

"Oh, it does make a difference, Miz Jessie," Zeb told her. "A whipsaw leaves little bitty scratches straight up and down on a board. Now a bucksaw, it leaves slanty scratches, and a go-around treadle saw, it makes curly ones. Anybody that knows lumber kin tell what kinda saw cut it, just by lookin' at it."

Ashmore echoed Jessie's opinion. He told Zeb, "Even if that's the case, it'd be hard to convince a judge and jury that you can identify a board that way."

"I guess my luck's run out, then," the old man said. "My location ain't no good, my horse and wagon's been stole, so even was I to cut some more lumber, I wouldn't have a way to haul it." Zeb stood up and turned to Jessie. "I thank you for listenin' to my troubles, Miz Jessie. And Ki, I owe you for helpin' me out back there on the road. But I guess I better start back now, and set down and figure what me and Wanda's goin' to do."

"Just a minute, Zeb," Ki said. He turned to Jessie and went on, "We're going to need shoring and facing lumber if you want Cliff to explore that new location. Zeb can produce what we'd want, and since there's no lumber for sale—"

"Of course!" she exclaimed. Then to Zeb she said, "Would you come and cut trees and make lumber for me, Zeb?"

"Why, sure I would, an' glad to, Miz Jessie!" Zeb grinned. "And it'd take a lot off of my mind, was you t' hire me." His face fell as he added, "'Cept I'd need a wagon t' haul my whipsaw over here from my cabin, and I ain't got one now."

"Don't worry, you're hired," Jessie told him. She stood

up and added, "We're going into town now for supper. You'll go and eat with us, of course. Then we'll go to the livery stable and I'll rent a horse and wagon for you to use until you can buy one. And I'll advance you some money until we can figure out what your pay will be."

By the time they'd reached Silver City and started down Broadway to the restaurant where they'd gotten into the habit of eating, the sun had dipped behind the Mogollon peaks. Though it was not yet fully dark, lights had started to appear in the store windows.

It was Silver City's supper hour, and the streets were virtually deserted. Out of habit, Jessie glanced at the small narrow building occupied by Mineral Developments. The door stood ajar, silhouetting the shapes of two men who stood at the edge of the street, as well as the lumber-loaded wagon and team that was in front of the building.

Before Jessie could call Ki's attention to the tableau, Zeb had jumped off the rump of Ki's horse and was halfway to the lumber wagon. Seeing him running across the wide street, Jessie, Ki, and Cliff followed him. They heard Zeb's shout as he reached the wagon.

"That's my load!" he yelled. "And damned if it ain't my rig and team, too!" He turned to the two men standing in front of the Mineral Developments office. "Now, which one of you's the sonofabitch that stole it?"

By this time, Jessie and the men had dismounted. They did not get to Zeb in time to keep him from closing in on the pair who stood beside the wagon. He'd grabbed each one by an arm and was shaking them and swearing at them in turn. Ki grabbed one of the men, Ashmore the other, while Jessie started trying to calm the angry Zeb.

"I say, what's this to-do about?" asked the man whose arm Ki was holding. "This gentleman and I were having a business conversation, and suddenly—"

"Just keep quiet for a minute, and you'll find out," Ki told his captive.

"Really!" the man exclaimed. His accent was British upper-class. "I must say, I'm not accustomed to being handled in this manner!"

Jessie had succeeded in calming Zeb by now. She led him to the others and said, "Now look at both of these men, Zeb, and see if you can identify either of them as one of those who attacked you and stole your wagon."

Before Zeb could speak, the Britisher broke in, "By Jove, this is the most extraordinary affair I've ever encountered! To be assaulted and accused of theft in front of one's own place of business!"

"I suppose you're in charge of this office?" Jessie asked him, nodding in a silent signal for Ki to release him. She realized that the Englishman was not likely to try to escape. She glanced at Ashmore and shook her head, and he tightened his grip on the man he was holding. Turning back to the Briton, she began, "I don't recall having heard your name yet, but—"

"Yes, quite," the man broke in. "Permit me. I am Gregory Benson. You, of course, are Miss Jessica Starbuck."

Jessie nodded. "I didn't see much point in crossing the street for a formal introduction. We both know quite well what our situation is."

"But that's really no reason why we should fail to observe the amenities, Miss Starbuck," Benson said, more than a hint of mockery in his voice.

"That's your choice, Mr. Benson," Jessie replied tartly. "But suppose we set aside everything else for the moment while we settle this question of Zeb's lumber and wagon."

"Settle, hell! One of them thieving bastards, or maybe both of 'em, is gonna be hauled off to jail, if I got anything to say about it!" Zeb growled angrily. He put his hand over his mouth, then removed it and said, "Beg pardon, Miz Jessie. I guess I'm so mad I forgot my manners."

"I think you're still a little too angry to settle this, Zeb," Jessie told him severely. "Will you trust me to handle things for a minute?"

Zeb nodded. "Shore. You ain't just a nice lady, you're a right smart one. Go ahead and talk for me. Jist don't fergit, I looked at them boards on the wagon, and they got my circle mark on the butt-ends of 'em. And that old nag, she'll answer to me quicker'n she will to anybody else, so there won't be no trouble provin' who they belongs to!"

Jessie turned to face Benson. Her eyes took in his appearance in two quick flicks. He was tall and solidly built, not fat, but inclined to look chunky in his thick Harris tweed suit. He wore no hat, and she saw that his dark blond hair was thinning, his forehead high, almost dome-shaped, in front. He had blue eyes, chubby clean-shaven cheeks, unusually full lips, and a stubby rounded jaw.

"Does this man work for you, Mr. Benson?" Jessie asked, indicating Ashmore's captive.

Benson shook his head. "I saw the chap for the first time a few minutes ago, Miss Starbuck. He came in and offered to sell me a load of lumber. I'd come out to look at it when your, uh, *associates* rushed up and attacked me."

Nodding, Jessie turned to the man Ashmore held. She held his eyes with hers for a moment, until the man turned away, then spent another moment sizing him up. He was young, in his middle twenties, she judged. Like most men in the rough backcountry, he needed a shave. He was dressed in the duck breeches and flannel shirt that seemed to be the standard prospector's and miner's garb. He wore an old army campaign hat, but without any insignia.

Jessie asked him, "Why did you bring that lumber here to this office after you stole it? Was it because somebody told you to, or did you just stop at the first likely-looking place?"

"Now hold on!" he said. "You ain't got no right to be askin' me questions! I don't see you wearin' no lawman's badge!"

"I think I agree with him, Miss Starbuck," Benson said quickly. "Marshal Nolan should be the one to ask the kind of questions you're putting to the lad."

"When I think I need your opinion, I'll ask for it, Mr. Benson," Jessie told the Englishman. "And in this country, nobody needs a badge to question a thief caught trying to sell what he's just stolen." She turned back to the young robber. "Now go on and answer the questions I just asked you."

Benson's intervention had apparently encouraged the captive to stay defiant. He snarled, "You can take your questions and go straight to hell, lady! I don't aim to say another word!"

Turning to look at Ki, Jessie raised her hand casually to her throat. She placed a forefinger at the neckline of her blouse and traced her fingertip up to the point of her chin.

Ki drew his *tanto,* the curved blade of the short knife glistening wickedly in the light cast by the open door behind them. A short step took him to where Ashmore and the man were standing. His face expressionless, Ki raised the knife and pressed its needle point on the captive's chin.

"I would advise you not to move your head," Ki told the man in a quiet voice, almost a whisper.

"Hey now!" the man mumbled, unable to open his mouth with the knifepoint anchoring his chin. "That thing's sharp! It can hurt a man!"

"Yes indeed," Ki agreed, almost whispering. "If you move and cause the blade to slip, it might cut off your head."

"Lady, won't you get this Chinee of yours to move his knife away?" the prisoner appealed to Jessie.

Jessie's voice held neither warmth nor sympathy as she said, "That will depend on how willing you are to talk."

"Oh, I'll talk, lady! I'll tell you anything you ask me!"

"Good." Jessie nodded to Ki. He removed the knife, but held it in front of the man's face, where it would always be in sight of his rolling eyes. She went on, "Suppose you start by telling us your name."

His voice subdued now, he replied, "It's Potter, ma'am. Sheldon Potter. Most folks calls me Shel or Shelly."

"Very good, if true. If it's not true, that's up to Marshal Nolan to find out," she said. "Now. Did someone hire you to steal this man's wagon and lumber?"

"No, ma'am," Potter replied. "There wasn't nobody put us up to it or paid us a penny. Me and my pals had a hard run of luck at our location. It just plain old petered out. We worked like dogs all last month, but we ain't dug no more carbonate than I can hold in one hand."

"So you decided to try robbery," Jessie prompted him when he fell silent.

"That's about how it was, lady. We was on our way to Silver City when we seen that old fellow there. Wasn't nobody around, and all of us knows what any miner in Grand County knows, lumber's so scarce right now it's worth more'n silver. So we made up to rob him. After we done it, we holed up off away from the road and waited till dark. I got picked to come in and sell the stuff, and—well, I guess you know the rest of it. Now that's gospel truth, and I'll swear to it!"

"I think he's telling the truth, Jessie," Ashmore said.

"So do I," Jessie agreed. "But hold on to him. We'll take him over and give him to Nolan. He can ride out and arrest the other two. It's his job to handle robberies, not ours."

"What about my lumber, Miz Jessie?" Zeb asked.

"Why, I'll buy that from you, Zeb," Jessie said promptly. "And the job of cutting more is still yours, if you want it."

Benson spoke suddenly. "I beg your pardon, Miss Starbuck, but I was the first person to whom this man offered the lumber. In business law, the first prospective buyer must reject an offer before the seller can offer it to another. The lumber is mine until I refuse to purchase it. However, I have every intention of buying it, so I'm afraid—"

Jessie broke in, "You're overlooking one vital point when you quote 'business law,' Mr. Benson. The man who made you the offer doesn't own the lumber."

"Now, I say, Miss Starbuck!" Benson protested. "Don't you think you're—"

Again Jessie interrupted, and this time her voice was sharply edged. "You may think all women are fools, but none of us likes to be treated like one. Go away, Mr. Benson. We have no business to discuss with you."

Benson's mouth hung open for several moments, and even in the uncertain light they could see the red flush of anger that crept up his face. Then he turned and disappeared into the Mineral Developments office, slamming the door behind him.

"I sure do thank you for standing up for me, Miz Jessie," Zeb said. "By cracky, I never seen a whop on the head turn into such a plug of luck in my life! Jist wait'll I git home and tell Wanda what's happened to us! I jist got a notion t' take off for my cabin right this minute, Miz Jessie, if you don't mind."

"Don't you think it would be better if you ate some supper first, Zeb?" she asked. "You've had a very hard day. In fact, it might be a good idea for you to stay here tonight and rest."

"Shucks, it takes more'n a little rap on the head t' keep a tough old codger like me down!" Zeb replied. "No, I thank you kindly for your invite, but if you don't mind, I'd rather mosey on home. Wanda's goin' to be—"

"Just a minute, Zeb," Jessie broke in. "How far is your cabin from the place where Ki found you?"

"Offen the road a ways, about two miles past where them fellers jumped me."

"Then that new location you and Ki are exploring is beyond Zeb's place, isn't it, Cliff?" she asked Ashmore.

"Yes. Three or four miles, I'd judge from what he said."

"Would you mind riding home with him, while Ki and I go and turn this Potter over to the marshal?"

"Of course not," Ashmore replied.

"Now, hold up a dern minute!" Zeb protested. "I don't need no help gettin' home! I know the way all right!"

"I'm not thinking about that, Zeb," Jessie told him. "I'm thinking about Potter's two partners. They're waiting for him somewhere along that road. You'd have trouble handling both of them if they attacked you again."

Zeb frowned. "Well, now, that plumb slipped my mind, Miz Jessie. But it's shore puttin' Mr. Ashmore to a lot of trouble."

"It's no trouble at all," the geologist said. "But I'm as hungry as a bear right now. We'd better follow at least half of Jessie's suggestion, and eat supper before we start."

"I reckon you're right," the old man said. "A leetle bit of time now ain't goin' t' make much nevermind."

"What about me?" Potter asked suddenly. "I guess I got some feelings too. I'm as hungry as you are. Do I get invited to go along with you?"

"You can look to the town marshal to feed you," Jessie told the youth coldly. She turned back to Ashmore. "Cliff, you and Zeb go across the street and eat. Ki and I will take this young hoodlum to Nolan's office. If we're not back by the time you're through eating, just go on with Zeb and we'll be waiting at camp when you come back."

After Ashmore and Zeb had started for the restaurant, Jessie said to Ki, "We'd better walk to Norton's office, Ki. I don't like the idea of Potter riding pillion with you. Go ahead. I'll lead the horses and follow right behind you."

Chapter 11

Broadway was dark now, except for the lights that spilled into the street from the saloons and stores. An occasional rider and now and then a wagon or cart passed them as they moved down the street. Ki kept a tight hold on Sheldon Potter's arm and Jessie trailed a few paces behind, leading the horses, keeping an eye on the prisoner. Pedestrians were scarce, and few of them paid any attention to the group, other than to toss them a glancing look. Most of them walked only as far as the distance from one saloon to the next.

Reaching the livery stable, they swung around it and saw the lighted windows of the marshal's office. A horse stood at the hitch rail in front of the door. Jessie wrapped the horses' reins around the rail and opened the door for Ki, who was still holding Potter's arm in his muscular hand.

Nolan swiveled around in his chair when he heard them come in. He was hatless tonight, and as Jessie suspected, his hair was coal black, worn shorter than was currently fashionable. His eyes slitted as he looked at the trio.

"I thought I told you to keep out of my way," he said to Jessie.

"I don't pay much attention to that kind of talk, Marshal,"

she replied, her voice even colder than his. "You should be thanking us instead of complaining. We've brought you a prisoner and saved you the trouble of hunting him down."

Nolan glanced at Potter briefly, then turned back to face Jessie and asked, "What's he supposed to've done?"

"A little highway robbery. Stealing a horse and a wagonload of lumber, attacking the man who owned the lumber," Jessie said.

"You're saying this happened here in Silver City, and I'm just now hearing about it?" Nolan demanded.

"He stole the wagon and lumber just outside town and had them in his possession when we captured him in Silver City, trying to sell the lumber," Jessie replied. "He confessed to the theft and to attacking the owner of the wagon. There were two other men with him in the holdup, and I'm sure you can persuade him to tell you how to find them. Now, what more do you want to know, Marshal Nolan?"

"A lot more than you've told me, before I lock him up on your say-so!" Nolan snapped. "So far, all I've got is a lot of talk from you! Besides, if I understand you right, if there was any crime committed—and I'm not real sure of that yet—it was outside my jurisdiction."

Jessie broke in quickly, "Unless I am mistaken about laws in the federal territories, Marshal, it's the duty of any officer to act when a crime is reported to him, wherever it may have been committed."

Nelson's eyebrows rose in surprise. "You got a degree from law school somewheres, Miss Starbuck?"

"No. Why?"

"Well, you act like some kind of jackleg lawyer, talking the way you do about the law," he growled.

"I just follow common sense, Marshal Nolan," Jessie told him blandly. "Which is what all laws should do, even if they sometimes miss the mark."

Nolan grunted sourly, then said, "Even if you're right,

I need a lot more than just a lot of words. What about witnesses? Evidence?"

"Oh, I'm sure there are enough of both to satisfy you," Jessie replied. "The man who was assaulted and robbed will testify. The horse and wagon and lumber belong to him, so you'll have evidence as well. And if you want a witness to his capture and confession, you can call on a Mr. Gregory Benson. I'm sure you're quite well acquainted with *him*."

Nolan's jaw dropped when he heard Benson's name, but he recovered quickly from the surprise and gazed poker-faced at Jessie while she stood waiting for his answer.

After a moment he said, "All right. Leave the man here. I'll look into the case and see if there's any reason for me to hold him. Now, if you two have told me all you know about this fellow, I've got plenty of other work to do. Close the door behind you when you leave."

As they mounted their horses to ride into town, Ki said, "I've got a feeling that the next time Nolan and Benson get together, our names are going to be mentioned more than once."

"I wouldn't take that bet, even if it was only for a penny," Jessie told him. "Alex always said the best way to weaken your enemies is to get them fighting with each other, and we've made a start in doing that this evening."

"I know I'd certainly like to be listening the next time they get together," Ki said.

They rode on around the livery stable and started up Broadway. They'd gone only a short distance when Jessie looked at Ki, frowning thoughtfully.

"What you said a minute ago has given me an idea, Ki," she said. "Cliff won't be needing you at the location for a few days, will he?"

"Oh, there's still some work I can do, but he can get along without me. Why?"

"Because I'd like as much as you would to know what

those two will be talking about. And if you use your *nin-jutsu,* I'm sure we can find out."

Since daybreak, Ki had been lying outstretched on the steep-pitched roof of the small, narrow building that had been squeezed between two larger ones facing Broadway. He'd begun his watch just after darkness began fading, carefully placing himself to avoid movement that would risk drawing attention to him.

Ki had chosen his position with the trained eye of a master of the ancient art of *ninjutsu,* and adapted himself to it with the mastery of the adept fighter that he'd become. Ki had not put on the traditional *ninja* costume, a form-fitting black suit like a coverall, with a hood that covered its wearer's head except for a narrow eye-slit. Ki's teacher, a very old, very wise master of Oriental martial arts, had impressed on him from the beginning of his instruction that the art of *ninjutsu* did not depend on a special kind of clothing, but on the *ninja*'s ability to fade into his surroundings.

You must learn to use every feature of the combat arena, the old man had said. *Train your eyes to see even the smallest things, the shapes and colors into which you can blend. Few of your enemies will have learned the lessons I shall teach you, to find the tiny dark corner in a room, the shadow of a chair, the uneven ground at the roots of a tree, the patch of mottled shade cast by sunshine through vines or branches on the earth or a roof or a wall. What the eye of one searching for you passes over without seeing will serve you as a shield."*

Inspecting the building, Ki had seen at once what he must do to avoid detection while he watched and listened. He lay with his head close to the stovepipe that ran through the back wall. Like so many of the semipermanent buildings erected hastily in Western boomtowns, the little structure had no chimney. The stovepipe had been installed with two

L-joints—the one that was connected to the stove inside the building angled through the wall, while the outside L was fitted with a piece of pipe that rose high enough to vent the smoke above the eaves.

Flattened out on the roof, Ki was almost invisible in the deep shadow cast by the taller buildings on both sides of the little shanty occupied by the cartel's agent. The light brown trousers and blouse he wore were almost the same color as the shingles on which he'd stretched flat. The position he had chosen allowed him to press his ear against the stovepipe that rose a few inches from the edge of the eaves. The pipe acted as a conduit, a speaking tube that funneled to him even the smallest noises from the room below.

Gregory Benson had arrived a half hour earlier. He had come in by the back door, using the space between the office and the adjoining buildings as an alley. If Benson had glanced up, he could have seen Ki's head in silhouette against the sky, even though the silhouette would have been broken by the outline of the stovepipe rising several feet above the eaves.

Watching the Englishman unlock the door only two or three feet below him, Ki had smiled inwardly. Again, the wisdom of his old master had been proved: *Choose a high place in which to hide,* he'd said. *Most people do not raise their heads above eye level. It is easier to turn the eyes down than upward.*

For a quarter of an hour after Benson's arrival, all Ki had heard was the rustle of papers, a chair scraping on the floor, and footsteps moving around in the small room. Once the cartel operative had scratched a match on the stovetop to light a cigar; the scraping of the match head on the metal top and the faint aroma of tobacco drawn up the stovepipe by the draft had told Ki what he'd been doing.

With infinite patience, Ki had waited. Now his wait was

being rewarded. Bootsoles grinding on the hard earth behind the building alerted him to the approach of the new arrival several moments before Tate Nolan turned into the space between the buildings and flung open the office door without bothering to knock. Like Benson earlier, the town marshal had not looked up. He'd gone into the office, and Ki had quickly pressed his ear against the stovepipe.

"What in hell was that Starbuck dame talking about last night?" Nolan demanded without even greeting Benson.

"D'you mind making yourself a bit easier to understand, old man?" Benson asked, his voice revealing that he was puzzled. "I haven't the foggiest about what seems to be upsetting you."

"She said you'd know some fellow that her and the Jap brought in the office for me to arrest," Nolan snapped. "He's supposed to've stolen a horse and a wagonload of lumber."

"Ah, of course. That fellow." There was a pause, and a whiff of burning tobacco brought to Ki by the wind told him that Benson was puffing on the cigar he'd lighted. Then the Englishman went on, "But I don't know the man, Tate."

"Then why'd she say you did? Damn it, if you've gone out and hired somebody else without talking to me about it, I've got a good mind to call off our deal!"

"Hold your temper while I explain, old chap," Benson said. "This lad they took to you came in here last evening and offered to sell me a load of lumber. I went out to the street with him to look at it, but before I'd a chance to do so, there were the Starbuck woman and her attendant and some old gaffer they called Zeb, raising a hue and cry about the lumber being stolen."

"And you'd never seen the fellow they say stole it?" Nolan asked. Then, suspicion in his tone, he went on, "You're sure you didn't hire him to steal it?"

"Oh, come now, Tate!" Benson protested. "'Pon my honor, I never saw the chap before!"

"All right," Nolan said, sounding only half-satisfied. "I suppose all she meant was that you'd been a witness."

"Which is precisely what I was," Benson pointed out.

"Let's let it rest, then." Nolan's shrug was expressed in his tone of voice. He went on, "What I really came to tell you is that I've finally got it fixed up for you to talk to one of the Apache war chiefs."

Benson grunted sourly. "You've taken long enough, I must say. What did you find out? Will he do the job?"

"Of course he will. I didn't expect him to say no. You're paying him to do what Apaches like to do best."

"Exactly what did he say?" This time there was distrust in the Englishman's voice.

"I didn't talk to the chief himself," Nolan replied. "I had to make do with one of his sub-chiefs. But he guaranteed that the chief will do your work."

"This chief's one of the more intelligent ones, I trust? I don't want one like some of the generals who are advising Her Majesty back home."

"You won't have to worry about this man. Nana is—"

Ki heard Benson's chuckle rise to a guffaw as the marshal stopped short. Then Nolan's angry voice cut in over the guffaws that came up the stovepipe.

"Damn it, what's so funny?" he grated.

"Really, old man!" Benson snickered. "Nana! That's what our babies call their nursemaids!"

"Don't let his name fool you, Benson," Nolan snapped. "I wouldn't advise you to poke fun at Nana. He's kept two troops of General Crook's best cavalry jumping like fleas on a hot griddle for the better part of two years now, and they still haven't cornered him or whipped him in a fight. Every time they think they've got him cornered, he just fades away and leaves the army looking like a bunch of fools."

Benson's laughter ended quickly, and his voice was serious when he asked, "How many men does this Nana command?"

"He's only got about forty warriors left now, but he knows how to use them. He's just the man you can depend on to do what you've got in mind."

"Are you sure?" Benson was businesslike again. "I want an Apache chief who'll do the job without attracting a lot of attention. I don't want him to attack Silver City, or storm across the area with a big band of fighting men."

"Damn it, I understand what you're out to do!" Nolan said impatiently. "Nana will too. It's the kind of fighting he's been doing all along. He makes quick surprise raids on a ranch or a little settlement, then he's gone before the word ever gets to Fort Bayard."

"And he'll follow my orders?" Benson asked. "I don't want the men working on all the locations to leave at the same time. All I expect the Apaches to do is make two or three raids a week on locations ten or fifteen miles apart. Can your Apache chief handle it the way I've got it planned?"

"That's up to you. If you tell him to do some damn fool thing, he'll more than likely walk out on you. It's going to be your job to handle Nana, not mine. I'll be too busy jumping from one raid to the next, cleaning up the messes he's made."

"For which I am paying you very generously," Benson pointed out quickly.

"And which reminds me of something," Nolan said. "How about the rifles I told Nana you'd pay him with? If they've got here yet, I haven't heard you mention it."

"They're on the way here. There was a telegraph message on the Lordsburg stage yesterday from one of our—" Benson paused, as though looking for an innocuous phrase to describe the cartel's tentacles. He found it and went on,

"One of our associated firms in Monterrey."

"You're getting the guns from Mexico?" Nolan's voice showed his surprise.

"It seemed advisable, Tate. They'll be smuggled over the border—not that it will take a great deal of effort, if I understand the situation to the south—and won't be as easy to trace as they would be if I'd gotten them from the East."

"When do you look for the guns, then?"

"They started from Monterrey ten days ago, and should get to Lordsburg the day after tomorrow. I've sent word by the stagecoach driver to my man there. He'll hire a wagon and haul them up here at once. They should be here two days after he gets the shipment in Lordsburg."

"Nana won't take your word they'll be here, you know," Nolan warned. "And if I was you, I wouldn't say anything to him about when they're coming in, or how. If you do, he's liable to ambush your man and take the rifles."

"Do you take me for a fool? I've handled enough contraband to know what to do."

"Nana won't make a move until he's got the guns."

"He'll get them, Tate. And a better bargain than he could expect. My associates bought six cases of twelve rifles each from the Mexican army warehouse in Monterrey, and the fifty rounds of ammunition I agreed to buy for each rifle."

"I didn't think you could find that many Winchesters loose in Mexico," Nolan said. "I had the idea you were getting them from somewhere back East."

"My associates couldn't locate enough Winchesters to fill my request. They had to refer my order to some mutual friends in Mexico. These are the French-made Mausers the Mexican army uses," Benson replied.

"Damn it, you promised you'd buy Winchesters!" Nolan said angrily. "The redskins don't like those Mexican Mausers!"

"Come off it, Tate," Benson snapped. "Your Apache

friends are beggars, they'll take any kind of rifles they can get. From what I've heard, they're always short of guns."

"Well, I suppose that's true, but—"

Benson broke in before Nolan could finish. He said, "I told you I'd deliver fifty guns to the Apaches. There'll be more than seventy in that shipment."

There was a long period of silence, and Ki could almost see an angry Nolan facing the Englishman. Finally Nolan said, "Well, I suppose Nana will take what he can get. He's likely tired of Crook's cavalry chasing him and his bunch, and figures to join the Apaches that've already gone into Mexico. But that's up to you to straighten out with Nana when you meet him. You're a slicker talker than I am, Benson, so maybe you can bring him around."

"Very well, Tate. Where and when do we meet?"

"There's a place on the old trail to Lordsburg, it runs to the west of the new road. I'll get you started on the trail, and you can't miss the place. There was a big landslide there once, and you can see where the slide cut off a side of a mountain when you're still a mile away."

"What time of day?" Benson asked.

"Tomorrow evening. You're to be there in the middle of the afternoon. That means the Apaches will be all over that place from daylight on, but you won't see any of them until they're sure you're not trying to trap them."

"What am I expected to do, then?"

Ki heard the scraping of chair legs on the floor, which told him that one of the conspirators, probably Nolan, had stood up. He found very quickly that his guess had been right.

"Wait until they show up," Nolan said. "Just be patient, and don't act like you're in a hurry. The Apaches will be there, and they'll show up when you don't expect them to."

"Where are you going, Tate?" Benson asked. "I counted on you going with me to meet the Indians."

"I haven't had breakfast yet, so I'm going to eat," Nolan answered. "Then I've got a few loose ends to tie up from my regular job, and as soon as I've finished that, I'll come back and show you where to find the old trail. Don't worry, Benson. I'll be back to get you started in time to make your meeting with Nana."

Ki waited only a few minutes after Nolan had gone before he rose silently to his feet. His rope-soled slippers made no sound as he took the two steps necessary to reach the edge of the roof. Then he dropped to the ground, timing his jump to the passing of a heavily loaded wagon on the street.

He made his way quickly along the rear of the store buildings to Bullard Street, crossed Broadway, and dodged behind the buildings on the opposite side of Broadway to make his way to Jessie's tent-office. His face was very sober as he walked along.

Chapter 12

"Didn't you leave your listening post a bit early?" Jessie asked when Ki pushed between the rear flaps of the tent.

"No. Nolan's come and gone. He won't be back until later. I've found out what he and Benson are planning, and it's not a good thing. I've been thinking how we can stop them, but I don't know enough about his plans yet."

"You sound so calm that I'm sure you've discovered something important," Jessie said, eyeing him closely.

"I did. Benson's getting ready to hire a renegade Apache band to start raiding the locations around Silver City."

"Why would he do that, Ki? There's nothing of any value at any of those mines. The men who are working the locations don't carry any money to speak of when they're on the job."

"He's not expecting to get money from raiding, Jessie. His idea is to create panic, to scare the miners so they'll want to sell out."

Jessie nodded slowly. "I should have thought of that. It's the kind of thing the cartel would do. But he can't expect all of them to sell to him. Some would come to us, and some would fight back and stick it out."

"I'm sure he's got some plans for us that he didn't mention to Nolan," Ki said dryly.

Jessie was silent for a moment, then said, "I'm afraid I've been underestimating Benson. His British manners and that highfalutin accent make him look and sound like a fool sometimes, but he's just as ruthless as any of the cartel's men."

"What he's planning is the sort of thing we can't guard against, Jessie," Ki said thoughtfully. "There are too many small mines, and the locations are too scattered."

"To say nothing of the country being too rough, and there being no way for anybody to know—or even guess—when the Apaches are going to strike," Jessie agreed.

"I'm sure of one thing," Ki told her. "They won't start making any trouble for at least a week. Maybe if we begin to spread the word now, we could warn most of the miners to be ready for trouble."

After a moment of thought, Jessie shook her head. "I don't think warning them is good enough, Ki. Most of the locations are worked by only two or three men, and some of the small ones are one-man mines. Even if they knew they were in danger of being attacked, they couldn't stand off a band of Apaches."

"We could notify the army, then," Ki suggested. "Fort Bayard's only a two-day ride."

"From what I've heard since we got here, there's never more than a single cavalry troop there. They keep most of the men out on patrol. One troop couldn't begin to cover all the locations that are being worked around here. Besides, you know how slow the army is to move."

Ki frowned. "There must be an answer, Jessie. We just haven't seen it yet."

They sat in silence for a few moments, then Jessie said, "Ki, you mentioned that the Apaches won't start raiding for a week or so, but you didn't tell me why."

"Several reasons," Ki replied. "One is that Benson hasn't closed a deal with them yet. He hasn't even met with the chief, and when he does, I intend to be there listening, so we'll know something about their plans."

"You said there were several reasons, though. What are the others?"

"For one thing, the guns."

"What guns?"

"Benson's paying the Apaches with rifles instead of money. The guns are on the way up here from Mexico. They're supposed to get to Lordsburg the day after tomorrow, and be delivered in Silver City two days later. That gives us three or four days to figure out what's best to do."

Jessie did not reply at once, then she said decisively, "We won't need three or four days, Ki. The Apaches mustn't get their hands on those rifles! We'll hold up the wagon before it gets to Silver City, and take the guns ourselves!"

"We'll have to know more about the shipment than we do now," Ki said thoughtfully. "And I don't think Benson will be foolish enough to tell Nana exactly when the guns will get here. I'm sure he realizes that if he did that, Nana would simply hold up the wagon and take them."

"I'm not going to make the mistake of underestimating him again," Jessie said. "But you've mentioned Nana twice. He's the chief of the Apaches, I suppose?"

Ki nodded. "They're Chiricahuas. From what Nolan said, it's a small band, only about forty."

"That's more than enough to wipe out a lot of locations. They'd hit and run, the way Geronimo and Victorio do, and even the army hasn't been able to stop them." After a moment she went on, "Benson must have the information about that gun shipment somewhere. It's up to us to find a way to get it."

Ki smiled. "I get the idea that you're planning a little burglary as well as some highway robbery, Jessie."

"I certainly am! Fighting the cartel's like fighting a war. They don't go by any rules, and we can't afford to, either."

"Oh, I'm not objecting, Jessie. But we'd better find out today what Benson's planning. If I was in his place, I'd want the rifles to get here at night."

"You don't think they might get here tonight, do you?" Jessie asked, her voice sounding worried.

"Not tonight," Ki replied. "If he had the rifles before that meeting he's having with Nana tomorrow, he'd go ahead and hand them over. Then we really would be in for trouble."

"You haven't said yet whether you know where and when they're meeting. You do know the place, don't you?"

"Not yet. I'm depending on Benson to lead me there."

"Is Nolan going along?"

"No. He knows the meeting place, though. All I found out is that the Apaches will be waiting somewhere south of town. Nolan told Benson that he'd show him how to get there, but wouldn't go with him to the meeting. I suppose they'll leave here together, and I'll be right behind them, of course."

"Then Benson won't be in his office tomorrow," Jessie said. "That's the chance I need. While you're following him, I'll be across the street, searching his desk."

"Good. With what I've found out so far, any information you might find could give us a real advantage."

"There's an advantage they have over us right now that I'd like to take away from them, Ki," Jessie said. "Right now we're vulnerable to the cartel in two places, the camp and the location. Wouldn't it be a good idea to cut that in half?"

"By moving the camp to the location?" Ki asked thoughtfully. "Yes, it would. With you here, and Cliff and me at the location, we're splitting our strength pretty badly."

"Shall we move today, then?" she asked.

"We can move right now, if you feel you can leave here."

"This office isn't as important to me as it was before you and Cliff discovered that silver lode. I don't want to give it up completely, but I don't feel as tied to it as I did when I first opened it."

"Then let's move camp this afternoon," Ki agreed. "We're both going to have enough to do tomorrow."

Moving the camp was a quick and easy job. Before sundown they had the tent pitched on a level spot a hundred yards from the limestone shelf that outlined the ledge where the mine would soon be started. It was a waterless camp, but Cliff Ashmore had promised that he'd try to locate a spot where Zeb could dig a well. The young geologist was a bit puzzled by Jessie's decision to move from the ridge, but accepted it without arguing.

"From the work that Ki's already done, I'm sure there's a big deposit of concentrate running back from that ledge," he'd told Jessie. "I think you'd be wise to start mining right now, if you intend to work it at all."

"I don't believe I could stand the idea of just letting all that silver lie in the ground, Cliff," she told him after a moment's thought. "Go ahead and put Zeb to work, and hire any other men we need to get the first shaft down."

"That's the one that'll tell the story, Jessie," Cliff said. "I'll start it in the middle of the ledge, and we'll work it straight back to the end of the lode. By then we'll know how really rich this location is."

"We'll need more help than Zeb to work on the first shaft, won't we?"

"Of course, but not until I can get started on a little stamp mill and a primary reduction setup. They'll just do on a larger scale what I did when I made the assay the other day."

"Go on and do what you need to, Cliff," Jessie told him.

"Ki and I have some things to take care of, but with a little luck, we'll be able to do them within a few days."

Riding into town shortly after daybreak the next morning, Jessie said to Ki, "When we started for Silver City, I didn't really expect to get into the mining business here. And I'm not sure I'd have told Cliff to start digging at that location, except for the idea that this mine would be something that I didn't inherit from Alex, something I did myself."

"Alex would be proud of you, Jessie," Ki assured her. "Not only for seeing an opportunity and taking it, but for all the other things you've done to carry on his work."

"I just wish he was still here," Jessie said, sadness in her voice. "I know you miss him as much as I do, and I don't know whether I miss him more at times like this, or when we're at the Circle Star. I really feel closer to him there than anywhere else, Ki. He loved the ranch so much."

"You're doing just what he'd have wanted you to."

"Oh, I know that. It's in places like this that we have to fight the cartel. If their plans to take over the West were to succeed, they'd have a mortgage on the future of our country."

They rode on in silence through the cool morning air. They reached Silver City and rode past the glow of red from the lanterns over the doors of the cribs, onto Broadway. At this hour of the morning the town was not yet fully awake. Along the street, perhaps a half-dozen horses stood patiently at hitch rails. As on most mornings, a few men slept propped up against some of the buildings, prospectors or miners who'd heard the owl's warning hoot too late and passed out, and had been dragged to the sidewalk to sleep off their liquor.

Some of those who'd left in time but had awakened early with hangovers were pushing through the batwings of their favorite drinking places for an eye-opener, and there were several clerks hurrying to open the stores before the proprietors arrived. Jessie and Ki pulled up their horses at the hitch rail of the restaurant a few steps from her tent-office.

They dismounted and were about to go into the restaurant when Ki glanced across the street at the little cabinlike building that housed the cartel's Mineral Developments front, and saw something neither he nor Jessie had noticed as they passed the place. Ki put a hand on Jessie's arm.

"Either Benson's earlier than usual, or he's spent the night in his office," he said, pointing to a thin, almost unnoticeable line of light that showed through a thin crack below the door.

"He's pulled the shade, too," Jessie said. She frowned and shook her head. "No. That window doesn't even have a shade. I remember noticing light coming from it when he's been there a few times after dark. Besides even when a shade's drawn you can almost always see a glow through it."

"He's up to something, then," Ki said. "Go on and have your breakfast, Jessie. I don't know what it means, but I'd better get over there right away and see if I can find out."

"Can you get on the roof without him hearing you?" she asked.

"Of course. I'll fasten one end of my *surushin* to the chimney of the store next door and go down hand-over-hand instead of dropping from the roof."

"Go ahead, then. There's nothing I can do to help you, but I'll tether your horse behind my tent before I have breakfast. If Benson looks across the street, he'll think I'm by myself as usual."

Ki hurried down Broadway to the end of the block and used the hand and footholds he'd found before on the back of the store next to the Mineral Developments office to mount to its roof. He looped one end of his *surushin* to the chimney that rose on the side of the store's wall and swung down carefully until he could plant the flexible rope soles of his slippers on the roof of Benson's office. Noiselessly he got into the position he'd learned was best when he'd used the metal stovepipe as his listening post. Benson was speaking when Ki placed his ear to the stovepipe.

"Now, before I begin explaining what you're here to do," the cartel boss was saying in his clipped British voice, "I want you men to keep behaving just as Gavilan instructed you to do before you started here. You are to act as though none of you have seen each other before. Is that quite clear?"

There was a murmur of voices from the room below. Ki could not distinguish between them, their murmur was too low and too subdued, but he guessed that at least a half-dozen men were assembled in the Mineral Developments office. Then one voice rose above the mumbling.

"All of us has been on this kind of job before, boss," the speaker said. "You don't need to worry none."

Ki's familiarity with the cartel's operations gave him the clue he needed. He could almost anticipate the broad scheme that Benson was getting ready to launch, even though he knew none of its details. He concentrated on the voices again.

"Very well," Benson went on. "Now, as to what your task is here, there are silver mines in the countryside around town. They are small operations, three or four men at most, often only one man. Within a few days, Apache Indians will be attacking them. You will stay out of the way of the Apaches. They cannot distinguish between you and the miners."

"We're gonna do the job on the town, I guess?" the man who had spoken earlier asked when Benson paused.

"No!" the Briton said sharply. "At least not now. That may come later. If it does, you will have adequate time to prepare for it. While the Apaches are attacking other mines, there is a Starbuck mine a few miles from town that you will attack. The Apaches will be told to stay away from it. If possible, I would like the Starbuck woman taken alive. There is useful information we can force from her."

"If we get that Starbuck dame alive, do we get a crack at her?" a fresh voice asked. "I tangled with her one time before, and that's something I'd sure like."

"Perhaps you'll get a chance," Benson replied. "She may need a bit of that kind of handling you'd give her to make her start talking. But I would not expect you to consider that a promise."

"What're we supposed to do while we're waiting?"

Ki recognized the voice of the man who'd started the questioning, and guessed that he must be either the leader or a self-appointed spokesman for the group. He strained his ears harder than ever to hear Benson's reply.

"Unfortunately, it was only yesterday that I found the Apaches will not be able to start their work as quickly as I'd planned when I sent for you. You will be free to do as you please for three or four days. But you must not draw attention to yourselves, and I will expect all of you to stay reasonably sober while we are waiting. Is that also clear?"

A new voice rose. "Does that mean we can't have a drink when we feel like it?"

"That is not what I meant at all," Benson replied. "Have a drink, but do not drink to excess."

"That means stay sober," another man said.

"Exactly," Benson agreed. "There is one exception to the rules I've just given you. At noon today, you will meet me on the road a mile south of town. By the way, I can't blame you for putting your horses in the livery stable when you arrived, but it was a stupid thing to do. I—"

"Nobody told us not to!" the man who'd done most of the talking for the new arrivals protested.

"I understand that, and Gavilan will answer to me for neglecting to give you full instructions," Benson answered.

"But when you go to get them, you will go to the stable one at a time. Do not ride out of town together. Bring your rifles as well as your revolvers. Find a place where you can watch the road without being seen by anyone passing. I will be riding with another man. Fall in behind us as we pass, and follow us. I'll brief you on your jobs while we ride to our destination."

"Are we gonna stay holed up in this pigeon coop till it's time to ride out?" one of the men growled. His was another new voice, Ki noted, adding to his mental tabulation.

"No," Benson replied. "Leave one at a time by the back door. Scatter when you reach the street. I promise you, the man who disobeys my instructions will regret it!"

"Don't worry, Mr. Benson," replied the man who seemed to be a semiofficial spokesman for the new arrivals. "We know the ropes."

"See that you stay inside them, then," Benson snapped. "Now, you, ah—what did you say your name is?"

Ki recognized the voice that replied as that of the man who'd done most of the talking.

"I'm Gomilla, boss. But most of the boys call me Gorilla."

"Really?" Benson asked, his voice icy. Then, with a bit more warmth, he went on, "Since none of you objected to Gomilla acting as your spokesman, I'm making him my second-in-command." He paused, and Ki could hear no objections in the muttering that followed. Benson said, "Very good. Gomilla, I want one man to stay behind this afternoon and keep an eye on my office. Whom do you suggest?"

"Well, Frankie's had a bad case of gripe-gut the last day or so. He'd be the one I'd pick."

"Very well. Frankie, come back here instead of going to the livery stable with your companions. I'll give you instructions then."

Ki pulled his head back from the roof's edge as the first

of the newcomers came out the back door. None of them looked up as they walked one by one between the buildings and disappeared in the alleyway. Ki counted six as the men passed below him, but his view of their backs gave him a few clues as to their origin. As the last one disappeared, he realized that none of them when alone would have drawn a second look in Silver City.

Four of them wore the duck trousers and flannel shirts that were so commonplace virtually everywhere west of Chicago. These four wore Stetsons: two of them were creased in the Dakota dimple, one was uncreased, Montana-style, and the fourth had a Texas line-crease in its high crown. The remaining two had on city suits. One wore a somewhat battered gray derby, the other a nondescript felt hat that could have come equally well from any city between New York and San Francisco.

Ki gave them time to reach the street, then climbed his *surushin* to the store's roof and went to the back corner, which was invisible from the office, and made his way to the ground. He hurried down the alley and crossed Broadway, and walked behind the buildings to the tent.

"I hope you learned something useful," Jessie greeted him.

"Very useful indeed," he told her. "Benson's brought in a half-dozen cartel plug-uglies to help him. And before I tell you what else I've learned, I'll give you the most important news. Stay away from the Mineral Developments office this afternoon. One of those thugs is going to be staying there as a guard while Benson's away. If you'd gone in there after we saw Benson leave, you might have been the cartel's prisoner two seconds after you opened the door!"

Chapter 13

Jessie showed no surprise, but looked at Ki and replied with a smile, "If you'll remember, Ki, I've done quite a bit of damage to some cartel gunmen in less than two seconds."

Ki smiled in return. "I made a bad choice of words. But I'm glad I could warn you, just the same."

"So am I. We're not ready yet to have an open fight with Benson and his men. Now what did you learn? I'm very curious."

"Quite a lot about some of Benson's plans, very little about the exact way he hopes to carry them out."

"As long as we know the plans, the rest will follow, Ki," Jessie said confidently. "Tell me just what he intends to do."

For the next quarter hour, Ki talked quickly and in concise detail, outlining most of what he'd overheard and drawing on his remarkable memory to repeat almost word for word the key points Benson had passed on to the cartel's hired thugs. When he'd finished, she leaned back in her chair and sat for a few minutes, thinking about what Ki had told her.

"Time is what we need right now, Ki," she said. "We'll

get that by grabbing the guns Benson has coming. He won't have much trouble getting more—the cartel has plenty of money—but he'll be forced to arrange for a new shipment. That'll take time, and so will getting the guns shipped here."

"His whole scheme might fall apart if Benson can't make good on his promise to the Apaches," Ki suggested. "They don't have much respect for men who break promises."

"Yes, but we can't count on the Apaches refusing to fight. If he can't give them weapons, he can offer them plenty of money to buy new guns for themselves after they've made their raids. There's a chance they'd settle for that, and we don't have much room for chances."

"Benson's not the only one who can offer them money, Jessie. But I suppose you've thought of paying them not to attack?"

"I have, but I don't like the idea. Whatever we offered to pay them, Benson would offer more. The Apaches are wily enough to take money from both of us. After they'd gotten paid, they might decide not to fight, but there's an equally good chance they'd go ahead and raid the mines anyhow."

"There's that, of course," Ki agreed. "Your first plan was the best. We can take the guns out to the mines and have Zeb dig a trench deep enough to bury them in."

"Wouldn't it be a better idea to distribute the rifles to the miners and prospectors, Ki?"

"Most of them have guns now."

"But not all of them have rifles," she reminded him. "Most prospectors and miners have so much gear to pack with them that they don't like to take on the extra load of a rifle."

"They'll be glad for us to give them one, then," Ki observed. "We'll have time to hand them around while Benson's waiting for a new shipment to be shipped in."

"We've still got the cartel's thugs to think about," Jessie

said. "He may be angry enough over losing the rifles to have those new men attack our mine."

"There are only six of them," Ki pointed out. "If you add Zeb to our bunch, we've got four. Those aren't good odds, Jessie. We've faced bigger ones before and won."

"Yes. I just mentioned that as a possibility we can't overlook. And I don't think we can plan too far ahead right now, Ki. Let's leave things as they stand, and go ahead with what we've decided to do."

Crouched behind a boulder on a high shelf overlooking the road from Silver City to Lordsburg, Ki waited for Nolan and Benson and the cartel plug-uglies to appear. The sun was high, and the spreading branches of an oversized pine that grew a few yards from the boulder cast a dapple of shadows over his vantage point.

Ki's clothing, a tan-colored shirt and trousers, blended almost perfectly with the hue of the boulder, as well as that of the rock outcrops that were a prominent feature of the parched landscape, and that of the earth itself. He'd taken the additional precaution of buying a short length of tan serge from one of the stores on Broadway, with which he'd fashioned a headcloth that covered his midnight-black hair.

One of the first lessons Ki had been taught as a student of *ninjutsu* was that during daylight hours, black is never found in natural outdoor surroundings except in areas of deep shadow. He'd also learned the obverse rule, that unless the ground is covered with snow, white is a color equally alien to the outdoors. The flowing lines of his loosely fitting clothing also helped to blur and soften the contours of his body. To someone passing on the road who glanced casually at the big boulder, Ki looked like part of the rock itself.

He'd been waiting almost an hour, and was prepared to wait another hour or more for the cartel operative and his companions. Ki's horse was tethered in a narrow arroyo fifty yards farther away from the road. He'd watered and fed the animal generously an hour or more before setting out, and knew that it would stand up to even the longest ride over the roughest ground.

Ki was getting ready to shift his position slightly when he heard the hoofbeats of horses approaching, and froze again. In a few minutes the riders appeared over a slight rise in the road, still a quarter of a mile away.

Benson and Nolan were riding a bit ahead of the cartel thugs. They were giving the horses their heads, letting them set their own steady, distance-eating pace. Benson was leaning toward Nolan, saying something to the Silver City marshal, who nodded curtly and gestured to his right. Ki took the move to indicate that Nolan was telling his companion that the place where they were to meet with Nana's Apaches lay somewhere to the west.

By the time the group reached his hiding place, Ki had frozen into total immobility. Benson and Nolan were not talking now, but they passed Ki without seeing him. So did the cartel's plug-uglies who followed them. They went by with a thumping of hoofbeats on the hard-beaten earth of the road, and when the two men at the rear of the little procession had gotten well beyond his hiding place, Ki went to the arroyo where his horse waited, swung into the saddle, and started riding after them.

Cover was scant on both sides of the road in that sparsely vegetated land. There were a few fairly thick stands of pine, and Ki used them skillfully, keeping a quarter-mile from the road and angling away from its curves as they serpentined down the slopes. Clumps of cedar were more plentiful, but Ki's head and shoulders showed above them when he rode erect in the saddle, so he spent much of his time bending low over the neck of his horse and raising his head only occasionally. He was content to keep the last riders in view as he followed.

He'd covered perhaps four miles when the horsemen ahead turned off the road. Reining in behind a cedar grove, Ki climbed out of the saddle and crept through the stunted trees until he could see his quarry clearly. They were moving almost due west.

For a moment he could not see the trail they were following, then he glanced ahead of the horsemen and saw it cutting over a hump a half-mile distant from the riders. At some time when the cartel group had been out of sight, Nolan had left them, for Benson rode alone at the head of the line of his thugs. Working his way back to his horse, Ki started riding at a slanting course that would bring him to the trail in front of them.

Ki toed his mount to a faster pace now. He also reined it to a different course, for the quick look he'd gotten at the short section of the trail ahead had warned him that it would more than likely wind in and out across the humps of the downward-sloping land, and he did not want the cartel's gang to see him.

He'd reached a lower altitude now, and even in the short distance he'd covered, the character of the terrain had changed, as it so often does in the mountainous areas of the West. Here the cedars were far more numerous than the pines, and grew much thicker, in bigger groves. As he rode, Ki flicked his eyes constantly across the landscape ahead, and it was his continuing vigilance that saved his life.

Skirting a cedar grove, he saw the tips of the trees ahead moving in a way that could not have been caused by the gentle breeze. Telling himself that the trees might be caught in a freak wind current, or that an animal may have been causing them to move, Ki nevertheless slid a *shuriken* from his shirt pocket. He was holding the razor-edged, star-shaped blade ready to throw when the Apache stepped out of the cedars a few yards ahead of him.

Ki's reactions took over. He sent the *shuriken* whirling

on its deadly mission with a quick, hard toss before the rifle the Apache was raising could be leveled and aimed. The blade traced a shallow, flashing arc in the bright sunlight as it spun past the butt of the rifle, which was already nearly to the man's shoulder, and sliced into the Apache's throat.

Grabbing at the embedded blade, the Indian let his rifle fall to the ground. He clawed frantically at the *shuriken* and finally dislodged it. A gush of bright arterial blood spurted from his neck. For a moment the Apache stared at Ki, his obsidian eyes widening to show their whites. Then he sagged slowly to the ground and lay still.

Ki reined his horse to a halt a few feet from the fallen Apache. Dismounting, he stepped over to the still-twitching body and looked at the man's face. It was decorated with two stripes of ocher paint on each cheek and a crimson stripe down the bridge of the nose. His eyes stared unseeing at the sky.

Knowing that the presence of the sentry was a sign that he must be close to the meeting place, and must move fast to reach a vantage point before Benson and his men arrived, Ki realized that he must advance faster and with greater caution. He broke off several cedar twigs and bunched them into an improvised brush to clean his *shuriken,* then dragged the Apache's limp body into the cedar clump and threw the rifle beside it. Then he remounted and rode on more slowly, scanning the landscape with even greater care than he'd used before. He looked now not only for other Apache sentries, but for a place where he could hide his horse.

After he'd ridden a short distance, Ki found the hiding place he needed. At some long-ago time, a tornadic wind had struck a stand of pine and twisted them like jackstraws as they fell. The pine trunks, stripped of needles and most of their branches, lay in jagged-edged heaps, with spaces like small nooks between them. Within a few minutes Ki had found two heaps that were both piled higher than the horse's back and had enough space between them to accommodate the animal.

Ki tethered the horse and climbed on top of the biggest heap of fallen trees. He stood almost motionless, as though he were a tree himself, shifting his feet slowly to turn his body as he scanned the slopes on all sides. A quarter-mile away, in a stand of pines rising near an oddly shaped conical boulder that towered man-high, Ki saw motion. He fixed his eyes on the trees and waited. As his vision adjusted to the sharp contrast between the sunny slope and the shaded grove, he was able to distinguish the forms of the Apaches gathered in the grove from the trees among which they had hidden.

Then he heard the thudding of slow-paced hoofbeats and looked away from the grove. On the slope, still distant from the grove where the Apaches were sheltered, Ki saw Benson's head above the tops of a cedar grove. He waited until he saw the cartel's thugs follow Benson onto the flat, then leaped from the heaped trees and began making his way to the stand of pines where the Apaches were waiting.

Twice as he neared his objective, Ki was forced to match his *ninjutsu* skills against the lifelong experience of the Apache sentries who had been posted to guard a broad perimeter around the stand of pines. He used the dense foliage of a cedar grove as cover to avoid being seen by the first one, but was forced to inch along on his belly, his tan clothing blending almost perfectly with the grassless, dun-colored earth, to get by the second man.

Ki reached the trees where the Indians were hidden just as Benson and his men arrived. The Apaches were watching the riders approach and did not see or hear Ki as he dodged from one tree to the next until he'd circled the back of the stand and curled his body around the boulder. He might have been part of the big upthrust rock as he lay motionless at its base.

An Apache stepped from the pines and held up a hand, palm forward. The man was painted as were the others Ki had seen, with ocher stripes on both cheeks and a vermilion streak along the bridge of his nose.

Ki tried to judge his age, but could not. He decided that the Apache could be any age, from sixty to a hundred. His long hair was gray, cut square at his jawline and held in place by a faded red cloth headband. He wore a loose blouse and high deerskin leggings, and his feet were encased in beaded moccasins. An oversized sheath at his hip held a bowie knife, and a Colt was holstered on the other hip. A rifle was held on his back by a sling that slanted across his chest.

Benson had reined in when he saw the Apache. He held up an arm to match the Indian's gesture and asked, "Are you Nana?"

Nodding deliberately, the Apache waited until he'd given Benson a thorough inspection before he spoke.

"Nana," he said. "You are man Nolan say want to talk?"

"Of course I am," Benson replied sharply.

"You get off horse. We look eye-in-eye when we talk."

Slowly and with obvious reluctance, Benson dismounted. Ki paid little attention to the Englishman; he was busy studying Nana's face. The first thing Ki had noted was that during their preliminary exchange of words, Nana's expression had not changed. It was as though he'd been carved from wood, with only his thin lips hinged to give an illusion of speech, and the words that came from them were flat and unaccented. His eyes were unreadable, without movement or depth. Benson, on the other hand, showed by his face and voice that he was angry, irritated, and impatient. The Englishman's traditional icy calm was totally absent.

Facing Nana, Benson said, "Nolan tells me you want rifles, and that if I give you guns, you'll order your men to use them the way I say."

Nana grunted sourly. "My men not do what you say. Do what *I* say. Nana is chief, not you."

"I don't want to give your men orders," Benson said. "But if I tell you what I want done, will you tell your men to do it?"

"How many guns you give?" Nana countered.

"More than you asked Nolan for."

Holding up his clenched fists, the old Apache opened and closed them four times. Then he said, "So many, I have said."

Benson nodded. He imitated Nana's gesture, opening and closing his fists four times, then said, "If you do a good job, I will give you"—again he clenched his fists and opened and closed them three times—"this many more."

If the Apache chief was surprised, he did not show it. He stared unblinking at Benson for several moments, then said, "What you want my warriors to do?"

"Nothing hard. Chase some miners away from where they're digging. Kill a few prospectors."

"Why you want this?"

"That's not your affair!" Benson snapped. "You and your men go out raiding whenever you feel like it. It seems to me you'd be glad to get new guns for raiding where I want you to."

Nana did not answer for such a long while that Ki could see Benson was getting restless. Unlike the cartel man, Ki understood the Indian's instinctive use of psychology in bargaining. His own people used the same techniques, and he'd observed that many Anglo-Saxons did not fully understand the use of calculated delay as a bargaining tool.

At last Nana spoke. He said, "You give bullets too?"

"Of course," Benson replied impatiently. "All you'll need to do your job."

"We keep bullets we not shoot?" Nana asked.

"You keep the guns and all the leftover ammunition,"

Benson agreed. "Now do we have a deal?"

"You give guns now, bullets too. We do," the Apache said.

"Good." Benson's voice was almost a sigh of relief.

"Where guns?" Nana asked.

"Not far. I can bring them here in two or three days."

"Must give guns now!" Nana insisted.

"Like hell I must!" Benson snapped. "I don't have to give you anything! Damn it, you'll do things the way I want them done, or you'll get nothing at all!"

When Nana spoke, Ki could tell at once that Benson's outburst had been effective. The old Apache chief nodded slowly, and his voice had lost its stridency.

"Is good," he said. "Three days. Here. You bring guns, tell who we shoot. We do this thing, we go."

"It's a deal," Benson agreed, extending his hand.

Nana hesitated for only a moment before grasping the outstretched hand. He shook it briefly, nodded, and said, "Is deal. Three days, here."

Without further ceremony, Nana turned and walked back into the pines, leaving Benson staring after him. Ki moved his head slowly, knowing that the attention of Benson and the cartel thugs would be concentrated on the Apaches. By the time Ki could see the stand clearly, his sharp eyes caught only a few flicks of motion as the Apaches departed.

"Where in hell did the bastards go?" Gomilla asked of nobody in particular.

Turning away from the grove, Benson shook his head. He said, "They simply faded away. Did you count them, as I told you to?"

"Sorry, boss," Gomilla replied. "All I seen was three or four little moves some of 'em made. But I guess their chief can tell 'em what they're supposed to do, all right."

"He'd better!" Benson snapped. "Well, we've done what we came to do. Back to town, you men. We'll see this place again when we deliver the guns."

Ki waited until the cartel crew was out of earshot before he moved. Then he leaped to his feet and began running toward the deadfall where he'd left his horse. The body of the dead sentry would be discovered when Nana gave the signal for the sentries to join the rest of the band, and Ki wanted to be on horseback and riding when they found the dead Apache's body.

He reached the horse just as the first shout arose from the cedar grove. He untied the reins and mounted and had covered almost a hundred yards in the direction of the trail before they saw him. Ki heard the menacing quaver of the Apache war cry rise, and looked back. Most of the Indians were still scattered among the trees, but a half-dozen were close behind him.

Ki tapped the big pinto's flanks with his heels, and the horse put on a burst of speed. The Indians began firing, but by now Ki was far ahead of them, and though a few of the slugs came uncomfortably close, none of them found a target.

A quavering yell sounded distantly. Ki glanced back. The Apaches were turning their horses, starting back to join their fellows. Ki let the pinto have its head for a few more minutes, but the horse had little desire left to run. He reined in slowly, and by the time they'd reached the road and his backward looks saw no sign of pursuit, he felt that he could rein in.

He let the pinto set its own pace going back to Silver City. The sun was low when he turned up Broadway and reined in at Jessie's office-tent.

"What did you find out?" she asked. "Did Benson make a deal with the Apaches?"

"He made the deal, all right," Ki said. "But whether it will hold up depends on his delivering the rifles he's promised."

"We'll start watching the road tonight, then," Jessie said decisively. "Now that we're sure of Benson's plans, it's up to us to stop him. And I'm afraid we're the only ones who can do it. If we don't, a lot of innocent people will be killed and Silver City will be thrown into a panic!"

Chapter 14

Jessie snapped fully awake the moment Ki's fingers touched her shoulder. She sat up, pushing aside her blankets, and strained to see his face in the darkness.

"Another wagon?" she asked.

"Yes. It's about halfway up the grade. It should be here in another ten or fifteen minutes."

"I hope this is the one we've been waiting for, Ki."

"This is only the third wagon that's passed at night," Ki reminded her. "If it's not hauling a rush shipment, I'm sure the teamsters would have stopped at dark, as most of them do."

Since Ki's return from the meeting between Benson and Nana the previous day, he and Jessie had been in a dry camp just off the road from Lordsburg. They'd left within an hour of Ki's return, delaying only long enough to buy the supplies they'd need, and to leave a note for Cliff Ashmore, telling him they'd be gone for a few days.

Riding south about three miles, they'd picked a spot at the top of a steep grade. Empty bottles, cigar butts, and piles of wheel-crushed horse manure told them that freight wagons hauling goods from the railroad or from the wholesale suppliers' warehouses usually stopped there to rest their horses and to stretch their own legs. In a boulder-strewn area a few steps away from which they could see the road clearly, Jessie and Ki had made their camp, and by dividing the night into shifts they had managed to inspect each freight-wagon heading for Silver City.

Most of the loads were easily identified at a glance, for in that arid country few teamsters bothered to stretch tarpaulins over their wagon beds. From their vantage point, Jessie and Ki could see the barrels, burlap sacks, boxes, and crates making up the load, and tell whether the wagon was hauling mining equipment or groceries or dry goods.

So far, none of the wagons had carried the long, shallow wooden boxes in which rifles were shipped, or the square boxes with DANGER stenciled on them in bright red that contained blasting powder or ammunition.

Moving through the moonless night to the roadside, Jessie and Ki reached the boulders they'd selected as their watch-points and hunkered down behind them. They could hear the creaking of the wagon and the thunking of the team's hooves and, as the wagon drew closer, the grating of its wheels and the high-pitched squeaks that came from strained leather harness straps. Then the wagon could be seen through the murk, moving snail-slowly up the final few yards to the top. It drew closer, and the watchers saw the shape of its load silhouetted against the night sky.

"This is the one we've been waiting for," Jessie said in a half-whisper when they saw the wagon's load silhouetted against the star-bright sky. There was no mistaking the long, narrow, shallow boxes that could only contain rifles, and the characteristic square boxes in which ammunition was shipped. "We'll wait until they stop. Take the other side, Ki. I'll handle this one."

Shadows in the silent night, they took their positions and waited for the wagon to reach the top of the grade. As it drew closer, they could hear the teamsters talking.

"Damned if I won't be glad to stop a minute when we top this rise, Murph. My back teeth's floating."

"Well, just hold on a minute longer, Frisco," Murph replied. "You know we can't stop till we get to the top. I was aiming to pull up there anyhow. I can do with a leg-stretch myself."

"Then how much further we got to go?" Frisco asked. "This seat's godamighty hard by now."

"Five, six miles. But don't forget what the boss said. We got to find this Benson fellow the load's consigned to, and start back as soon as he's got the stuff off the wagon."

"Damned if I'm gonna start back before I git some shut-eye! We ain't been outta this wagon more'n an hour or two for goin' on three weeks, Sam! If I'd've knowed how long this haul was gonna take us, I never would've took it on, extra pay or no."

Instead of replying, Frisco called, "Whoa, boys! Whoa!"

Ki and Jessie heard the creaking of harness and the ratcheting of the brake being set. Before the teamsters could get off the high seat, Jessie had planted a booted foot in the stirrup-step on one side and had the muzzle of her Colt jammed into the temple of the man nearest her, while Ki had levered himself up on the opposite side and was touching the point of his *tanto* to the throat of the driver. He pulled the teamster's revolver from its holster and tossed the weapon to the road.

His voice cold, Ki commanded, "Get out of the wagon."

"All right, all right!" Murph said quickly. "There ain't but a dollar or two in my jeans pocket, but I'll hand over what I got without making no trouble."

Ki glanced across the wagon and saw that Jessie had gotten the other wagoneer started moving. He told the man on his side, "Don't give us any trouble, and you won't get hurt." Then, as the teamsters' boots hit the roadbed, he went on, "Now walk over to where your friend is."

"We ain't got no notion to argue with you, mister," Frisco said. "Take our money and be on your way."

Jessie had already taken out the leather bootlaces they'd had the foresight to buy when they stocked up at the store. She was busy securing Frisco's wrists behind his back. Ki took one of the laces and quickly tied Murph's wrists in the same fashion, and when told to bring their ankles together so that they could be tied, the wagoneers obeyed without arguing. The two men having been secured, Jessie went to get the horses.

"We won't gag you," Ki said. "There'll be teams passing by when it's daylight, and a couple of hours here won't hurt you."

"Whatever you say," Frisco agreed.

Murph said, "Fighting wasn't part of the deal when we taken on this job. All we get paid for is hauling freight." He hesitated for a moment, then went on, "But there's one thing I'd sure like to find out before you go."

"What's that?" Ki asked.

"Is that a boy or a woman with you? There's times I think it's one, and times I think it's the other, and I'll be damned if I can figure out which."

Smiling inwardly, but keeping his face straight, Ki told the teamster, "I'm just going to let you keep wondering, Murph. It'll give you something to think about while you're waiting." He turned away and went to the wagon, where Jessie was tying the horses' reins to the tailgate. In a few moments the wagon was rumbling on toward Silver City.

"I'd say we've made good progress since we pulled Benson's fangs, Ki," Jessie said.

They were standing beside the well that Zeb had finished

digging a few hours earlier, watching the water grow clear as the mud and debris of disturbed earth settled slowly to the bottom.

"We have," Ki agreed. His mind still on the new well, he went on, "I'll use some of the boards we have left to build a casing for this tomorrow or the next day."

Jessie nodded. She was looking over the location. The well was its newest feature, though it had changed in other ways. The tent still stood where it had been pitched when they moved the camp from the ridge, but now it was used only by Ki and for storage. In a pit below the tent, the rifles and ammunition Jessie and Ki had captured from the cartel lay buried, hidden by a foot-thick layer of dirt. A rude cabin, its boards still shining bright yellow, stood a short distance from the tent.

Jessie and Cliff Ashmore occupied the cabin, an arrangement that had come about tacitly and without discussion. After all their years and adventures together, Ki had needed no hint from Jessie to volunteer to stay in the tent. He'd seen the attachment blossoming between Jessie and Cliff, and would no more have commented on it than Jessie would have remarked on Ki's private life.

Part of the load of lumber bought from Zeb by Jessie after its recovery had gone into the cabin's construction, part to the rolling-trough in which the concentrate from the lode was reduced to a uniform texture. The dome of the little adobe *hornito* that Ashmore had built for his assay work stood near the trough.

There were two new features on the face of the ledge. One was the pole-gate that Zeb had constructed to close a crevice that ran back from the ledge to provide a corral for the horses. The other was the framing around the mine's adit. The remainder of what had been a good-sized lumber pile had shrunk to a few boards, the rest having been used to shore up the interior of the exploratory shaft. It was now more than twenty feet long and growing longer daily, due to steady digging by Cliff Ashmore and Zeb.

"I still feel like the man who was waiting to hear the other shoe drop," Jessie said. "I keep wondering where he is and what kind of trouble he's planning."

"He has been invisible longer than I'd thought he'd be," Ki agreed. "We haven't seen him since the day after we grabbed the cartel's rifle shipment, and that was nearly three weeks ago. He must've known it was us who took the wagon, and I'm as surprised as you are that he hasn't tried to get the rifles back."

"I'd almost welcome having him around, Ki. If he makes another attack, it could be our chance to finish smashing the cartel's schemes."

"I'm sure your guess about him was right," Ki told her. "He's probably in Lordsburg, where he can send telegrams and get quick answers to them."

"I saw Nolan on the street when I was in town yesterday," Jessie said. "Benson seems to have left him in charge of the cartel's thugs. There were two of them with him."

"We both know the cartel doesn't give up easily, Jessie. It won't be long before we'll have to fight again."

"I know. But I keep wondering about Nana's Apaches. They have short tempers and long memories."

"If they're still around, they've kept out of sight. We'd certainly have heard about it if they'd raided any of the locations or been up to any other mischief," Ki said. "Or even if they'd been seen by a prospector."

"Keeping out of sight until they're ready to stage a raid is one of the things Apaches do best," Jessie commented.

"I'm not forgetting that, Jessie. But it seems to me that our best bet is to keep going the way we are now, exploring the lode and keeping our eyes open."

"Of course it is," Jessie said. "And that's just what we'll do—as long as the cartel lets us alone."

They saw Ashmore emerge from the mineshaft, followed by Zeb. The two men walked over to them and the geologist asked, "How does the new well look?"

"Still a little bit muddy, Cliff, but it's clearing fast," Jessie replied.

"I told you I'd know where to dig, Miz Jessie," Zeb said. "This ain't the first well I witched out in these parts."

"You did a fine job of water-witching, Zeb," Jessie said, smiling. "Ki and I tested the water, and it's sweet and good."

"Well, I'm right glad, Miz Jessie. Now I got a favor to ast. I got a mizzly bunch of chores t' do at my place. Reckon I could get here afore sunup t'morry and put in a long day, then take off the next day while I catch up at home?"

"If Cliff doesn't need you, I certainly don't mind," Jessie replied.

"It's all right with me," Ashmore said. "Zeb, if you'll get here early tomorrow, we'll make a few feet more shaft, then I'll do my assays while you haul the concentrate out. Then I'll put in the next day at the rolling-trough. I can handle that alone, and Ki can probably give me a hand if I need some help."

"Of course, Cliff," Ki volunteered. "I'll do better than that. I'll try to get the well-casing job finished tomorrow, and when Zeb takes his day off I'll handle the work he usually does."

"Now that's right nice of you, Ki," Zeb said. "Maybe I can get Wanda to bake you up a pie and bring it to you when I come back from my day off."

"I'm sure we'd all like that," Jessie said. "Speaking of Wanda, Zeb, when are you going to bring her over for a visit?"

"Well, I keep asking her to come along with me, but she jist backs off. I reckon you know how it is with little girls, Miz Jessie, they're a mite shy about strangers sometimes."

"I wish you'd think about moving over here to the location, Zeb," Jessie went on. "I've told you before that I'll be glad to pay for the lumber if you want to build a cabin here."

"Well, that's right nice of you, Miz Jessie, but I guess it's best if I stay where I am. It ain't much over a half-mile, now that I sorta beat a leetle trail so's I don't have t' use the road no more. I'll think on it some more, and maybe change my mind about moving, later on."

"You do that," Jessie said. "Anytime you change your mind, we'll all pitch in and help you move."

When Zeb had gone, Jessie turned to Cliff and asked, "How did the shaft go today?"

"Still the same, Jessie. The lode doesn't show any signs of petering out, and the carbonate looks as good as ever. I'll know more about it when I run my next assays, but I'm more and more certain that you've got a real rich strike here."

"Well, good news is always welcome, Cliff. Now suppose we clean up and ride into town for supper. There's not enough in the grub box for a decent meal, so we'll have to buy supplies as well. And I'm anxious to see if we can get any clue as to what's happened to Benson."

"He's been gone for quite a while now," Ashmore said.

"Yes. Ki and I were talking about that a minute ago. We're both sure he's working up something new. But we may not find out what it is until he starts stirring things up again. Then all of us might have to forget about mining and start fighting."

Cliff Ashmore came out of the mineshaft and squinted at the morning sun. It was clear of the horizon, its rays beginning to creep down the face of the limestone outcrop. He saw Ki walking toward the new well, carrying the boards he'd need for its casing.

Ashmore walked over to the well and said, when Ki

came up, "I'm beginning to wonder what's happened to Zeb. I started earlier than usual because he said he'd be on the job before sunrise, but he still hasn't shown up."

"That's not like Zeb," Ki replied. "He usually gets here earlier than this."

"Oh, I'm sure he has a reason," the geologist said. "But I'm at the point where I need him to help me."

Jessie came out of the cabin, saw Ki and Ashmore, and came over to join them. "You're both early birds," she said as she came closer. "And since you didn't wake me up to fix breakfast, I'll bet you're starved by now."

"More worried than starved," Cliff told her. "Zeb still hasn't shown up."

"But he said he'd start work before sunup, and Zeb's always been here when he's said he'd be," she said. "Do you think he was taken ill after he got home last night? Or that his little girl might be sick?"

"We hadn't gotten far enough to do anything but wonder," Ashmore replied.

"If you don't mind waiting for breakfast, I'll ride over to his cabin and find out," Jessie offered. "He mentioned yesterday evening that he's coming to work on a trail that cuts out the long ride around by the road."

"Yes, I remember," Ki said. "But Zeb's the only one who's used the trail, Jessie. None of us know it."

"I shouldn't have any trouble finding it," she told Ki. "It wouldn't be the first new trail I've puzzled out. There's no reason for either of you to interrupt your work. I'll saddle Sun and go see what's keeping him. There must be something wrong, or he'd have been here when he said he would be."

Jessie had Sun saddled and was on her way within a few minutes. Like Ki and Ashmore, she'd noticed the direction Zeb had been taking lately when he left the location at the end of the day, and had no trouble picking up the hoofprints of his horse.

Because the hard-baked earth did not always show hoofprints well, Jessie traveled more slowly than she would have on a road or a well-marked trail. The prints led her in a winding course that detoured around rises and the thick groves of cedars, but ran in a straight line through stands of widespaced pines and across rock outcrops and barren ground.

Jessie was nearing a cedar grove when she heard the first shots. She reined Sun to a halt when the first report sounded from the far edge of the grove just ahead. With a quick move that long practice had made almost instinctive, she slid her rifle from its saddle scabbard and sat listening. For a few moments there was silence, then an answering boom broke the still air. The second shot was from a gun of heavier caliber than the first; it boomed in a deep basso instead of the sharp crack of one of the new light-caliber rifles that were replacing the .50- and .60-bore weapons of an older frontier.

To Jessie's experienced ear, the first shot had come from a new rifle, probably a .40-.60 Winchester, to judge by its report. The second had sounded like a .58 Springfield or a .52 Sharps. There was a great difference between the flat, rolling boom of either of the older guns and the higher-pitched report of the new lighter-caliber Winchester.

Cradling her own rifle ready to use, Jessie waited. She was sure now of what was taking place ahead of her, but many lessons in strategy from Alex and Ki, as well as her own adventurous life since Alex's murder, had instilled in her a large store of battle wisdom. With the craft of a seasoned campaigner, she took time to orient herself and judge the odds before rushing into an unknown fight on terrain that was equally strange.

In the distance another rifle barked, and it too had the crack of a modern gun. Jessie still did not move. When she heard the shot fired in reply, she was sure her deductions had been correct. She toed Sun into motion, and reined him around the perimeter of the cedar grove as another exchange of shots shattered the stillness.

Chapter 15

When Jessie turned Sun and began skirting the cedar grove, she was responding to the chain of deductive reasoning that had flowed in an instant through her quick, logical mind: For about a half-mile she'd been following the new trail Zeb had beaten, so his cabin must be very near. His rifle would be an old big-bore weapon; the cartel's men would have newer guns. Zeb not only worked at the Starbuck mine, he'd offended the cartel's local boss. Adding one fact to the next formed a chain leading to Jessie's immediate conclusion that Zeb had been chosen as the first victim of what she was sure marked a new offensive thrust by the cartel.

Jessie realized that in reaching her conclusion she'd been guided only by intuition, but the experience she'd gained during years of battling the cartel told her that she was correct. The same quick logic also told her that by circling the cedar grove to get between two of the attackers, she risked being caught in their crossfire, but risk had never stopped her from acting before, and it did not stop her now.

At the side of the grove, Jessie slipped from the saddle. "Stand, Sun," she told the big palomino, knowing he would not leave the spot until she commanded him to. With her Winchester held ready for instant action, she continued circling the cedars on foot, watching and listening.

Only a few minutes had passed since the double exchange of shots. The early-morning air was silent as Jessie moved with the stealth of a stalking lioness around the dense foliage of the thickly bunched trees.

After she'd advanced a dozen steps, she could see one corner of the cabin, and another few steps revealed the back of the little dwelling and its surroundings. It stood on bare ground between the cedar grove and a stand of pines. A few paces to one side of the unpainted planks that formed the cabin walls there was the low wooden casing of a well. Beyond the well stood a small slat-sided stable, and Jessie immediately recognized the horse inside as Zeb's. Though more proof was not needed, his wagon stood beyond the stable. There was one small window in the cabin wall, pointed shards of its glass pane still remaining in the frame.

A rustling in the grove drew Jessie's attention from the cabin to her own situation. She studied the cedars, looking for signs of movement in their thickly interlaced branches, but everywhere she looked the branches were motionless.

Another shot cracked from the pines beyond the cabin, but it drew no answering shot. Jessie saw a wisp of gunsmoke in the pines, and through it she got a quick glimpse of a man's form dodging behind one of the trees. She had a fleeting impression of a painted face, a headband, and Apache-style rawhide leggings, but by the time she'd brought up her rifle, the man had vanished behind the tree trunk.

It's Benson's work, all right, Jessie thought. *He's back, and he must've brought more rifles with him to bribe the Apaches. We made a mistake, not looking for Nana's band more carefully. They've probably been hiding all this time in the mountains south of town, where Ki saw them talking to Benson. Now we're going to have a real fight on our hands!*

To her left, the rustling in the cedar grove began again, and Jessie turned away from the cabin to look once more at the dense growth. The tips of some of the low-growing trees were moving gently, and some of those closer to her were beginning to shake. Jessie dropped to the ground and lay flat, her rifle ready. Lying prone, she could see into the grove along the ground, though the bottom branches of most of the trees sagged into the tan soil and limited her vision to only a few yards.

One of the ground-scraping branches began bending. Jessie shouldered her Winchester and watched the branch over its sights. The branch grew still, but she did not move. A shot rang out, this one from beyond the stable. From the cabin, Zeb's answering shot boomed. Jessie looked up, but the stable and wagon lay between her and Zeb's target.

Directly in front of her, less than twenty feet distant, the cedars shook and feet scraped on the hard earth. Jessie looked toward the sound, and saw a man standing at the edge of the grove, his rifle shouldered. His gun roared, but as Jessie raised her Winchester to get him in its sights, he dropped to the ground.

Lowering the rifle's muzzle, Jessie fired through the trees. A yell of pain came from the man, then she heard his footsteps thudding and fading as he ran at a slant toward the stable. He staggered and ran unevenly, but he was moving fast. One of his arms was dangling limp, the other grasped his rifle.

Jessie swung her rifle, but before she had time to aim, the big-bore gun roared from the cabin window, and the man dropped. Beyond the cabin, a short volley of shots rang out from the pine stand and from the rifleman stationed past the stable. Jessie looked at the pines and saw the sniper she'd glimpsed before. He stood in plain sight now, aiming his rifle at the cabin.

Swinging around quickly, she snapshot. The rifleman's body jerked and he fell. Jessie lowered the Winchester's muzzle. The man she'd shot began rolling toward the protection of the pine trunk that he'd used as cover. Another report boomed from the cabin as Jessie tried to get the wounded man in her sights, but he was moving with the speed of desperation. She squeezed off a second shot, and the slug kicked up dirt only inches away from him as he reached the protection of the tree trunk.

Jessie eyed the stretch of bare ground between her position and the cabin. She'd heard shots from four different rifles, and had been able to judge the position of the attackers beyond the cabin from the sharp reports of their rifles.

They were stationed in an arc around the opposite side of the little structure, two almost directly in front of the cabin, the other two spread wider apart, beyond its corners, where they could cover each end. She could see no way to cross the exposed strip without becoming an easy target. Even if she belly-crawled across the barren spot, she would be visible to the snipers at both ends of the arc.

While she still lay prone, debating her next move, knowing she must make it quickly, Jessie heard the distant thudding of hoofbeats on the hard earth. After she'd listened for a moment or two, she fixed the position of the sounds: They were coming from the area past the cabin, beyond the stand of pines.

Jessie's instinct told her that the attackers were giving up the fight, discouraged. She was sure the man Zeb had shot was dead, and was equally sure she'd wounded another. Her sense of caution warned her that the cartel's thugs might be using the horses as decoys, having one man move them noisily while the remaining three held their positions. She thought for a moment, trying to find a way to determine which of her conclusions to believe, and an answer soon came to her.

Tugging at the chin strap of her wide-brimmed, low-crowned hat, Jessie tilted the barrel of her Winchester and placed the hat on the muzzle. She lifted the rifle slowly, with frequent pauses. There were no shots from either end of the cabin. She raised the hat still higher, extending her arm until the inviting target rose above the tops of the low-growing cedars. Still the morning remained quiet.

"Zeb!" Jessie called.

After several moments, Zeb replied from the cabin window, "That you, Miz Jessie?"

"Yes. I think they've gone. Can you see or hear anything from the front?"

"Nary a rizzle. I heared them hosses movin', and I got a hunch you're right," he replied.

"Cover me as well as you can, then," Jessie told him. "I'm coming to your cabin."

"Come ahead. I'll keep my eyes peeled."

Jessie dashed for the cabin, expecting at any second to hear a rifle bark, but no shots broke the stillness. Encouraged, she slowed to a walk when she was sheltered behind the structure. She glanced at the still form of the man Zeb had killed, lying facedown on the bare ground, and what she saw made her stop in her tracks. The dead man was lying with his arms extended. A coating of dun-colored dust was on his hands, but the sleeves of his blouse had worked up when he fell, to disclose a strip of white skin.

Bending down, Jessie turned the man's head to look at his face. It too had been smeared with dust before he'd added the touches of paint on his cheeks, and his hair had the fine texture of an Anglo-Saxon's, not the coarseness of an Indian's The rifle he'd dropped when he fell was a brand-new Winchester, still bearing streaks of the grease applied before it was shipped from the factory. Jessie did not recognize him, but she'd never gotten a close look at any of the cartel thugs who'd come to Silver City to help Benson. He was one of them, of that she was sure.

Miz Jessie?" Zeb called. She looked up and saw him standing at the corner of the cabin. He came over to her, and when he'd looked at the corpse he exclaimed, "Why, that ain't no blamed Apache, even if he is got up t' look like one!"

"No, he's not," Jessie replied. "And I'm sure the others weren't either. But we can talk about that later, Zeb. Let's go inside."

Entering the cabin, Jessie took in its single sparsely furnished room with a glance. It had windows in all four walls, but they were small and admitted little light, though the panes had been broken out of all of them. Narrow bunk beds stood at each end; there was a cast-iron cookstove in the center of the back wall, and a tall wooden cabinet at one side of it. A second cabinet stood on the other side of the stove. The center of the room was occupied by a table and four chairs, and a bureau stood to one side of the door.

From somewhere in the room a small voice asked, "Pa? Is it all right if I come out now?"

Jessie looked around, but saw no one.

"Sure it is, Wanda," Zeb said. "Come right on out."

Jessie had discovered the source of the voice by now, and was looking at the bunk when Wanda crawled from below it. She stared at Zeb's daughter with almost unconcealed surprise.

From his remarks, she'd expected to see a toddler-aged child, but Wanda was at least in her late teens, perhaps a year or two beyond them. She was as tall as Jessie, and much sturdier in her proportions. Her shoulders and hips were broad, her bust generously full, her features regular and attractive, but somehow just short of beautiful. She had long black hair that was tied at the nape of her neck with a ribbon and streamed down her back. Jessie suppressed a frown as she studied Wanda's full oval face, and saw a look of mature wisdom in the young girl's eyes.

"This here's Miz Jessie Starbuck, Wanda," Zeb said. "You heard me talk about Wanda a lot, Miz Jessie. This is her, my little girl."

"But—" Jessie was staring at Wanda, having expected a child instead of a mature young woman. "But, Zeb, I expected her to be a little girl, not much more than knee-high."

"That's how Papa thinks about me, Miss Jessie," Wanda said with a smile. "And I'm right glad to meet you, he's talked about you and Ki so much."

"And I'm very pleased to meet you, Wanda," Jessie replied. "We'll have time to visit together later, but right now there's something I've got to talk about with your father." She turned to Zeb. "Those men are gone now, Zeb, but if I hadn't come looking for you when you didn't show up as early as you said you would, they might've killed both you and Wanda."

"Oh sure, I know that, Miz Jessie. And I'm right thankful to you fer showin' up when you did."

"Thank me later, Zeb, if you still feel like it after I've said what's on my mind," Jessie told him. "I've invited you before to move to the location. Now I'm going to insist that you move. This cabin's too isolated for your safety. This time I'm going to insist that you move."

"But—" Zeb began.

Wanda interrupted. "Miss Jessie's right, Papa. You and me might be dead now, if she hadn't come along. I don't want you killed, any more than I want to die myself. Tell her yes, please do!"

Zeb looked from Wanda to Jessie and saw only determination in both their faces. He'd lived too many years not to know when he was on the losing side. He nodded slowly. "I guess you're right, Miz Jessie. We'll move over there in a week or so."

"You'll do it right this minute," Jessie said firmly. "You and Wanda can have the tent—I know Ki won't mind moving. And as soon as possible, you can build yourself a cabin there." She turned to Wanda and said, "I'll help you start packing what you'll want to take, while Zeb gets the wagon ready."

"I think it's awful nice of you to take the time to help me, Ki," Wanda said, turning to flash him a smile as they jounced on the seat of the wagon.

Ki smiled in return and replied, "All of us want to help you and Zeb, Wanda. We're glad to have you at the mine."

"But you've been good to me and Papa from the start, moving out of the tent so we'd have a place to stay, and sleeping in that old, dark, dismal mine instead."

"It's dark, but not dismal, Wanda," Ki said. "It's warm and comfortable. I've slept in a lot worse places."

"Well, with Papa so busy, I still think you're nice to help me move some more of our things," she said. "I just wish there was room in the tent for our cookstove, so I could bake you a cake or a pie or something like that."

"Wait until Zeb's built your new place," Ki told her, pulling up the horse in front of the cabin that Zeb and Wanda had lived in before Jessie insisted they move. "Then you'll be able to cook whatever you want to."

Zeb and Wanda had been living in the tent at the location for almost a week now. For the first two or three days, Wanda had stayed out of sight, then she began leaving the tent to watch when jobs such as sifting the concentrate to remove limestone chips and working the sandy ore in the rolling mill brought the men out of the mine. She'd had little to say, and had been careful not to get in their way, but Ki had been aware of her presence. He was aware of her presence now, as they went into the cabin. Wanda went to one of the bunks and sat down.

"Is something wrong?" he asked.

"No, I just want to sit here and rest a minute after that bouncing around in the wagon. Why don't you come rest, and we can decide what we want to take back to the mine."

Ki sat down beside her. He glanced around the bare little room, surveying its contents, and when he turned back to Wanda, he was surprised to find her staring at him. On an adult's face, her expression would have been called a thoughtful frown. Then her face cleared and she smiled at him.

"I was just wondering about you," she said.

"I won't ask what you were wondering," Ki said. "You might be shy about answering."

"I'm not really shy, Ki," she protested. "Not when there's just me and somebody else talking. You're the one who's acting shy, like you never were alone with a girl before."

Ki realized that Wanda had talked to him more freely during their brief trip from the location than she ever had before. He said, "Tell me what you were wondering about, then."

"I was wondering what Japanese men are like," she replied.

"Just like any other men, I suppose, except for our eyes."

"You're not different anyplace else?"

"Not that I know of. We might look at some things a little differently, that's all."

"That's not what I mean," Wanda said. She laid her hand on Ki's crotch. "I mean down here."

Ki was not usually surprised. This time he was. He took

Wanda's wrist and tried to lift it away from him, but she closed her hand, holding him firmly. He said, "I don't think that's a thing for us to be talking about."

"Oh, Ki!" Wanda shook her head, smiling. "Don't treat me like a baby! I'm not, you know. I know what American men look like, but not Japanese. Are you bigger or smaller?"

Ki was not easily surprised, but Wanda's unexpected question startled him, and his face showed it. Before he could stop himself, he asked the first question that popped into his mind. "How would you be able to tell?"

"I told you I'm not a baby," she answered. "I've seen lots of men with their pants off. I know what they look like down there, and I know how it feels when they put it inside of me. I know how I feel, too, when they do that. I like it."

"If you're trying to joke with me, Wanda, you're not doing very well," he said. He still had a loose hold on her wrist, but Wanda brushed his hand away with her free hand and began to fondle and feel him. Ki recognized the touch of experienced hands, and realized that she was telling him the truth.

"Stop now, Wanda," he said. "Pick out the things you want to take back to the mine and I'll load the wagon. That's what we came here to do."

Wanda said pleadingly, "Please, Ki! Papa's kept me out here away from town so long that I haven't been near a man for two or three months, and it seems like a year! Please, Ki!"

Wanda no longer looked like a young girl. Her widened eyes looked eagerly from his face to the bulge at his crotch, which her busy fingers had begun to create. Her full breasts were heaving, her lips moist and quivering as she kept up her manipulations. When Ki realized his words were having no effect, he grasped her wrists firmly and removed her hands. He got to his feet, and Wanda gazed up at him with a plea in her eyes.

"Now let's get busy," he said firmly. "You show me the things you want to take back, and I'll put them in the wagon."

Wanda sighed. "All right, Ki. But just because you pushed me away this time doesn't mean I'm going to stop trying."

Chapter 16

Jessie swung off Sun and tossed the palomino's reins to Ki as he dismounted and came up to her. They glanced around the location. Wanda had gone back to her earlier habit of staying in the tent most of the time after her effort to seduce Ki had failed. Zeb was nowhere in sight, but Cliff Ashmore was hunkered down at the assay oven just outside the mine adit. The ledge behind him was bathed in its own shadow as the sun dropped toward the horizon. He put his work aside and joined them.

"What's the news from Silver City?" he asked.

"Everything's quiet," Jessie replied. "Too quiet. The Mineral Developments office is closed, and there wasn't any sign of Benson and his thugs. We did see Nolan swaggering down Broadway, but he went into a store the minute he saw us."

"They're licking their wounds, I suppose," Ashmore said.

Ki nodded. "Either that or waiting for reinforcements. But we don't want to relax, Cliff. It's been only a few days since Jessie drove them away from Zeb's place. We've got a long way to go before we're out of the woods."

"I've been keeping as close watch as I could," Cliff told

Ki. "If there was anybody prowling around, I didn't see them."

"Ki and I agree that when they attack, it'll probably be at night," Jessie said. "But after that beating they took at Zeb's cabin, I'm sure they'll lie low for another few days. And when they show up, all of us know the plan we'll follow."

During the short span of daylight that remained, the day's chores were finished, supper eaten, and dishes washed. Zeb wasted no time in going to the tent and to bed, and Wanda followed him as soon as she'd finished washing the dishes while Jessie dried. Then Jessie and Cliff strolled away arm in arm, as lovers will, and vanished into the shadows. Left alone by the dying fire, Ki strolled to the improvised corral and made sure the horses' water pail was full, then went into the mine. In the midnight blackness of the shaft he spread his bedroll, undressed, and slipped naked between the blankets.

Sleep came to him quickly after the long day, but even when tired, Ki slept lightly. The soft whisper of feet on the sandy floor at the mine entrance roused him and he woke, fully alert as soon as he'd opened his eyes. His hand reached under the edge of his bedroll and grasped one of the *shuriken* he always kept there when he slept. Holding it balanced to throw, Ki sat up and swiveled around to face the entrance. Then he relaxed when he saw Wanda silhouetted against the lesser darkness outside.

"Ki?" she whispered softly, before he could speak.

"Yes, Wanda," he replied.

"I couldn't go to sleep," she said. "Can I come sit down and talk to you a little while?"

Ki did not reply for a moment, then, "All right," he said. "If you'll promise just to talk."

"That's all I want to do. I'm lonesome, Ki. Papa's always too tired to talk to me, and everybody else is too busy."

Wanda felt her way along the rough wall until she was close enough to see the dark rectangle of Ki's blankets against the light-colored sand of the floor. Sitting cross-legged in the center of his blankets, Ki watched her moving toward him. His eyes were adjusted to the almost pitch darkness by now, and he could see as she drew closer that Wanda wore only a thin shift or nightgown. She stepped over to the bedroll and sat down on its edge.

Ki still held the *shuriken* in his hand. He started to tuck it away under his bedroll, but even in the faint ghost of illumination that trickled from the adit, the shimmer of its bright steel was visible.

"What's that?" Wanda asked.

"It's a *shuriken,*" he told her. "One of my weapons."

"Like a knife?"

"A little bit. It's really designed to be thrown."

"I don't really understand about it, Ki. Can I feel it?"

Ki passed her the *shuriken,* saying, "Handle it carefully. It's very sharp."

"You hold it, then, and I'll just feel of it."

Ki held the star-shaped blade, and Wanda extended her hand to touch its cool, polished surface. Her exploring fingers moved too near one of the needle-sharp points, and involuntarily Ki took her hand to keep her from cutting the finger. His movement as he leaned forward brought his bare chest brushing against her arm.

Wanda gasped and forgot about the *shuriken*. She twined her arms around Ki in a tight embrace that held his upper arms pinned to his body, and found his lips with hers. Before Ki could break her embrace, she'd thrust her tongue into his mouth and it was darting about, seeking his.

Ki realized that what was happening had been almost inevitable since their encounter a few days earlier at the cabin. He'd not allowed himself to be aware of the number of times since then when he'd looked at Wanda speculatively, and then banished from his mind the fact that he was wondering about her.

He let himself sink back as Wanda pressed the full weight of her body against him. Through the thin shift, he felt the firm nipples of her generous breasts rubbing his chest. Then Ki was lying on his back, Wanda's body warm and soft against him, her lips still clinging to his, their tongues entwined.

They lay without movement for several moments, and then Ki felt Wanda's hand go to his crotch and grasp his beginning erection. He still made no move to stop her or to free himself. Nor did he try to pull away from her clinging lips to protest, or move to lift her away when Wanda's warm, stroking hand had brought him fully erect and she lifted herself to straddle his hips and sink down on the erection she'd created. Wanda broke their kiss and pulled her head back to look at Ki's face.

"You aren't going to scold me again and make me stop, are you, Ki?" she asked. "I know you don't want me, but that doesn't keep me from wanting you."

"I'm not going to do either one, Wanda," Ki replied. "All I want to do now is share all the pleasure we can together."

He lifted her shift over her head to bare her breasts and kiss them. Wanda gasped and squirmed, and thrust her hips down harder on Ki's lean, muscular body while his warm, moist tongue moved over the erect tips of her soft breasts.

As he prolonged his caresses, Ki felt her generous body twist and shiver, then she suddenly began to groan softly and tremble. The trembling grew to a fury of twisting, and he realized that she'd already reached an orgasm. He held her close to him until her spasmodic jerking faded and died away to soft contented sighs.

"Oh my!" Wanda breathed. "I didn't want to finish so soon, Ki!" She sank down, rested her head on his muscular shoulder, and whispered, "But you didn't finish as fast as I did. And I know you're not through yet, because you're still in me and filling me up like nobody else ever has."

"I'm glad I'm pleasing you," Ki said. "I suppose I was wrong when I scolded you the other day, but you're so much like a little girl—"

Wanda broke in to say peevishly, "I haven't been a little girl for a long time, Ki. I know I'm not smart like Jessie is, but girls learn about men real young when they live in the places where Papa and I have been. But I don't want to talk about that now. Aren't you ready to start again? Because I am."

"Yes. I was waiting for you."

Ki held Wanda to him while he lifted her and rolled them both over to reverse their positions. He began stroking, gently and in a slow deliberate rhythm. Wanda's muscles were softly relaxed at first, but after several minutes they began to grow taut. Ki recognized the silent signal of her body, and speeded the tempo of his deep penetrations.

When he felt Wanda growing taut, he slowed down and continued at a gentler pace, but his slowing did not delay the onset of her next shivering spasm. She was taken suddenly when it arrived, and cried out with a happy sob while she rolled and thrashed below him and urged him to thrust harder. Ki did not obey until long after her orgasm had faded. Then he speeded up, and released the tight control he'd kept on himself.

"Faster, Ki! And deeper!" Wanda urged as he began to lunge with greater force. "I know I'm going off again, and I want you with me this time!"

Ki was approaching the verge himself. He lunged with quick, hard, triphammer strokes that brought high-pitched cries of pleasure from Wanda and added to his own building desire to reach his peak.

Ki relaxed his control and thrust in a series of quick, hard lunges which brought him to the climax that was already shaking Wanda. With a sigh of fulfillment he fell forward on her soft breasts as his muscles relaxed.

"Oh, Ki!" she sighed, wrapping her arms around him and clasping him close as they lay quivering in the waning throes of shared ecstasy. "I thought I knew something about men. But now that I've been with you, I know I'm just beginning to learn."

"We'll learn from each other," Ki promised. "There'll be other nights, and longer ones for us, Wanda."

"Tonight's not over yet," she said. "And I don't want it to be. Let's rest awhile, Ki, and start all over again!"

Ki and Wanda had only two uninterrupted nights together before the cartel struck again. Jessie had made it her job to go into town daily, to keep an eye on the Mineral Developments office and watch for signs that a new attack was building. She returned on the third day with her face sober and her usually full and smiling lips pressed into a thin hard line.

"We can expect them to strike any time now, Ki," she told him when Ki volunteered to carry her saddlebags into the cabin so they could have a brief private conversation. "There were a lot of ugly-looking strangers hanging around Benson's office today. The office was so full there wasn't room for all of them inside. I got a glimpse of them when he opened the door a moment."

"I don't like that a bit," Ki said. "If you remember, Jessie, whenever the cartel lets its men parade openly, they've planned some dirty move they're sure will win for them."

"I was thinking the same thing on the way back from town," Jessie said.

"We've been expecting it, of course," Ki went on. "And

whatever they've planned won't take us by surprise."

"No, but if you have anything left to do, finish it up as fast as you can," she told him.

"I'm as ready as I'll ever be, Jessie. I've been working on the arrangements all day for the past three days, you know. It will take about an hour for Cliff and me to put on the final touches."

Jessie looked at the sky and said, "That's just about how much daylight we have left. You go ahead and work with Cliff. I'll warn Zeb and Wanda to be ready."

All those at the mine went to their usual sleeping places in the few minutes before darkness fell. They'd been careful during the last hour or two before sunset to follow their usual routines, in the event that a cartel spy was watching. Jessie and Cliff went to the cabin, Zeb and Wanda to the tent, Ki to the mine. They left no fires burning, did nothing out of the ordinary that might warn an observer.

Once out of sight, no one left the places in which Jessie had asked them to stay, though the tension of waiting gnawed at their nerves. Even Jessie and Ki felt the strain, in spite of the victories they'd won over the cartel and its plug-uglies in the past. The hours dragged on and midnight passed, then slowly trailed until daybreak began. In the east the sky faded to gray and the gray brightened to silver. Soon the rim of the horizon glowed pink with the flush that comes before dawn.

During the later hours of the night, Jessie and Cliff had taken turns napping until Jessie realized she could see Cliff's features in the growing light. They kissed and moved behind the logs Zeb had felled at opposite sides of the pine stand.

In the tent, Zeb had snored while Wanda kept watch, her nerves too taut for sleep, until the time came for him to take his position, then Wanda shook him awake and they made their way in the dim gray light to the corral.

In the mine, Ki had not slept. Appointing himself the all-night watcher, he'd placed his blanket just inside the entrance. Then, folding his legs under him, he placed a supply of matches on the blanket at his side, and waited with stoic calm until the dawn crept in.

As soon as there was enough light to use a rifle sight, the cartel's minions attacked. They swept down the slope from the road with a thunder of hooves, twenty horsemen, hard-faced killers recruited by the cartel from outlaw hang-outs, hired guns used to fighting battles that meant nothing to them except a stack of gold eagles if they survived.

Tate Nolan was in the lead, and Benson rode at the rear. As they galloped into the wide stretch of open ground between the limestone ledge and the pine stand beyond it, they began peppering the tent and cabin at once with volleys of rifle-fire. The slugs from their Winchesters tore through the cabin's boards as easily as they ripped through the canvas of the tent.

Jessie fired the first shot, her signal to the defenders to pick targets and start shooting. She picked the nearest riders as her targets and fired methodically, while slugs from the rifles of the cartel thugs were being wasted on wood and canvas.

Zeb's old .52 Sharps spoke with its basso roar from the shelter of the corral. He was not a silent marksman. When one of his shots went home in a horse or a man, he shrilled a hoarse victory yell.

At the back of the clearing on the side opposite Jessie's position, Cliff Ashmore shot horses rather than their riders until a bullet from one of the cartel's hired gunmen plucked at his shirtsleeve. Then he forgot his qualms and aimed higher.

Ki, alone in the mine entrance, did not fire at all. His rifle leaned against the wall, within reach, but he had another job to occupy his attention. Stretched in neatly formed bundles on the floor in front of the blanket were the fuses he and Cliff had spent so much time measuring to precisely the same length and laying in narrow, buried trenches to the dynamite planted in a triangle in the center of the clearing.

Shouts had risen from the cartel's raiders as the hidden rifles began speaking, but they did not realize at once that they were caught in a crossfire, bunched in the lines of fire laid down by the mine's defenders.

Tate Nolan was the first to grasp what was happening as the horses began neighing shrilly and rearing in panic and the first of the cartel raiders fell from their saddles.

"Scatter out!" he shouted, trying to make his voice heard above the din. "Stop bunching up!"

If any of the attackers heard him, they did not or could not obey. The horses were not trained to stand gunfire. Two had fallen, and three were riderless. They started milling inside the lines of fire laid down by the defenders, plunging and bucking, the shrill neighing of those that had been wounded creating still further panic among the others.

Ki waited until he saw that the cartel crew was bunched as tightly as it would ever be. He struck a match and touched it to the three lines of fuse in quick succession. The fuse was timed to burn at a quarter of a minute per foot. The hot sparks zipped through the hollow core and touched off the explosive. Under the horses' flailing hooves, the ground heaved and red flashes flared up to envelop horses and riders as well.

Some of the horses were tossed high, and fell to the ground with crippling force. Others reared with such frantic fear that they toppled back, fell on their riders, and crushed them. Most of the thugs who managed to stay in the saddle did so by letting their rifles drop and clinging to their saddlehorns with both hands. Some of those who had been wounded by the deadly triangle of dynamite were limping or trying to get to their feet. Almost half of them lay still and would never rise again.

Nolan was one of those who had lost his rifle but stayed in his saddle. He saw Jessie rise from behind the log that had sheltered her and wheeled toward her, his hand sweeping down to draw his Colt. Jessie cut him down with a single shot as he dragged the gun from its holster, and he toppled from his horse and lay still.

Benson had turned his mount toward the road even before the dynamite exploded. The blast caught his horse under its belly and lifted the cartel boss out of his saddle. Scrambling to his feet, he looked back at his motley crew. A glance told him he had been beaten. He started toward a riderless horse, but a rifle slug kicked up dust at his feet. Then Benson saw the mouth of the mine, and ran toward it.

Ki saw him coming. Rising to his feet, he sent a *shuriken* whirling toward the running man. The blade sliced into Benson's throat just below his jawbone. He clawed for a moment at the star-shaped blade that was embedded in his flesh, blood welling between his fingers. Then his knees buckled slowly and he lurched forward. He staggered ahead a few steps, and fell. The effort he made to get up drained the scant strength he had left. He pitched to the ground and lay still while a pool of blood formed a red halo around his head.

After the gunfire and the dynamite blast, the whinnying of horses and the groaning of wounded men sounded faint in the quiet air. Jessie walked to the corner of the cabin. Ki met her there. Ashmore was making his way slowly toward them, and Zeb and Wanda were just emerging from the corral.

Jessie looked at the remnants of the cartel's raiding force—the dazed horses, the still forms on the ground, and the shallow craters torn by the dynamite.

"I'd say we've got some cleaning up to do, Ki," she

said, her voice holding no elation over their victory.

"It won't be that bad. I'll have the surviving plug-uglies do the dirtiest work," he said.

"Yes," Jessie agreed. She was silent for a moment, then went on, "As soon as the work's done, I'm going to put Cliff in charge of the mine. When the lode's worked out, I'll tell him to close it down."

"What if it's the mother lode?" Ki asked.

"I don't really care, Ki. I have enough; I don't need or want any more. We've beaten the cartel, stopped them for a while, at least. That's what really matters. Let's finish up in a hurry. I'm ready to go home to the Circle Star."

Look for

LONE STAR AND THE AMARILLO RIFLES

twenty-ninth novel in the exciting
LONE STAR
series from Jove

coming in January!